WARMING FIRES

Stories for All Seasons

WARMING FIRES

Stories for All Seasons

BY JEFF KUNKEL

Enjoy!

FACE TO FACE BOOKS
Mount Horeb, Wisconsin

FACE TO FACE BOOKS is a national imprint of Midwest Traditions, Inc., a non-profit organization working to help preserve a sense of place and tradition in American life.

For a catalog of books, write:

Face to Face Books / Midwest Traditions
P.O. Box 320
Mount Horeb, Wisconsin 53572 U.S.A.
or call 1-800-736-9189

Warming Fires
©1997, Jeff Kunkel

Book design: MacLean & Tuminelly

Cover Artwork is from a watercolor by Steven R. Kozar, titled "Winter Evening Reflections," ©1995 Steven R. Kozar. For more information about original landscape paintings or limited-edition prints by this artist, contact Wild Wings, P.O. Box 451, Highway 61 South, Lake City, Minnesota 55041-0451, or the Kozar Gallery, Mount Horeb, Wisconsin.

Library of Congress Cataloging-in-Publication Data

Kunkel, Jeff, 1954–
    Warming fires : stories for all seasons / by Jeff Kunkel.
       p.   cm.
    ISBN 1-883953-21-9 (hardcover : alk. paper)
    ISBN 1-883953-20-0 (softcover : alk. paper)
    1. Middle West – Social life and customs – Fiction. I. Title.
PS3561.U53W37   1997
813' .54 – dc21   97-16081
                                                                 CIP

First Edition

10 9 8 7 6 5 4 3 2 1

for Mary Elyn

PREFACE

My FATHER'S FAMILY immigrated from Germany to Milwaukee, Wisconsin, where they became city people and business owners. My great-grandparents, Frederick and Catherine Kunkel, bought a family summer home on Pewaukee Lake, a Queen Anne Victorian with eight bedrooms and a porch which caught every puff of lake breeze like a sail. This home became a gathering place for many generations of Kunkels on summer weekends. Each evening, we gathered on that porch and told stories, so I learned much about my relatives and about good storytelling.

My mother's family immigrated from Germany to Kiel, Wisconsin, and became country people – farmers or ministers. My grandparents, Oscar and Mathilda Kazmeier, owned and worked a seventeen-acre farm on a bend of the Sheboygan River. The farmhouse, built by my grandfather, had an enormous front room, dining room, and kitchen, and served as a gathering place for many generations of my mother's family. Each summer, I spent much time on this farm, and during winter holidays, my grandmother cooked for twenty or thirty. There was lots of churchgoing, cardplaying, and storytelling. As a teen, I learned to farm, hunt, fish, and trap in the farm country around Kiel.

I lived with my brother and parents in Brookfield, a suburb of Milwaukee where the city met the country. My father was a salesman for General Foods Corporation, and my mother was a nurse. I attended the University of Wisconsin in Milwaukee, where I majored in English and learned to practice good writing and enjoy stories from many other eras and cultures. I was expecting to go on to law school, but during my senior year, I experienced a sudden and unexpected spiritual awakening which made me change course. I attended Garrett-Evangelical Seminary in Evanston, Illinois, and learned the ancient stories of scripture and tradition, and I began to write fiction. In 1980, I received a Master of Divinity degree and ordination as a United Methodist minister.

I left Wisconsin to pastor a church in California – the first Kunkel to leave Milwaukee since the Kunkels first arrived in Wisconsin. As pastor, I have heard much private storytelling and have come to view preaching as public storytelling. I return to Wisconsin at least once a year. On one of these visits, I met the woman who became my wife, Mary Elyn Bahlert. We married in Milwaukee, and I have come to know the fine storytellers of her Wisconsin family.

Two years ago, I wanted to give myself fully to writing and artmaking, so I took a sabbatical. Now, I am Director of Music and Children's Programs at Walnut Avenue United Methodist Church in Walnut Creek, California, and a full-time writer and teacher of writing workshops.

Warming Fires is a collection of short stories with a vivid sense of place and memorable characters. Each story is carried by a distinct voice and unfolds with humor, action, feeling, and surprise. The characters – farmers, ministers, industrialists, teachers, hunters, newlyweds, children, and animals – get into trouble, and this trouble creates an opening, an occasion for fear or faith, awareness or action, both in the character and in the reader. God moves through these stories in a free and unpredictable way as "the One with whom we have to do."

I have read the stories in this collection to congregations, groups, classes, and assemblies, and I have learned much about the stories through the honesty, generosity, and good sense of these audiences. I am especially grateful to the readers who helped me shape and strengthen these stories for publication – Paul Hessert, Sandy Bails, Bob Ditter, Judy Wheeler, Janet Riehl, my editor Phil Martin, members of my writing group, and Mary Elyn Bahlert, my wife and friend.

I hope these stories become "warming fires" for you, lighting up the night, crackling, flaring, glowing, shooting sparks, warming flesh and blood.

Jeff Kunkel
Oakland, California
Vernal Equinox, 1997

THE STORIES

THE GREAT NORTHERN TRAIN WRECK

LIKE MOST NEWLYWEDS, Glenn and Karen did whatever it took to postpone their first fight. He bought her the diamond ring she wanted, even though it cost him twelve hundred, twice what he wanted to spend. She took his last name, Schneider, even though she grieved the loss of her maiden name, Winton, and would have kept it if she thought he would have consented. He got married in her church, Good Shepherd Lutheran, even though he wanted to be married outdoors, by a river or lake. She, a city girl who could not swim and did not fish, honeymooned at his Thunder Lake log cabin. Later, she told her bride's maid, "By day, I sat in a wobbly, leaky boat and untangled his fishing lines. By night, I listened to mice and godknowswhat scamper under our bed while we tried to youknowwhat." But there comes a moment when that first fight needs to be allowed, suffered.

Karen set her fork on her dinner plate and asked Glenn, "Apple pie?" Chewing his last piece of pot roast, Glenn nodded. She took away his empty dinner plate and replaced it with a pie plate, and on it, a quarter of a pie with a scoop of vanilla ice cream on top, leaning, melting. Karen folded her hands on the table, took a deep breath, and said, "I'd like to go to a show this Friday."

Glenn looked at her and blinked, startled that she had suggested a change in their Friday night routine: her at home, him at the Club. Glenn loved his Friday evenings apart from Karen and had come to count on them, but he did not want to say this directly, so he waved his fork like a wand and said, "You go ahead and have fun."

Karen took the handle of the gravy-boat spoon and stirred the dark, heavy gravy. Finding a lump, she squashed it with the back of the spoon blade and said quietly, "I don't want to go alone."

Glenn took his first bite of pie, chewing, thinking, swallowing. "Maybe Cheryl can go."

"I don't want to go with Cheryl. I want to go with you." Glenn was about to suggest that they go to a show on Saturday night, but Karen added, "We haven't been together on a Friday night since your honeymoon."

"*My* honeymoon?" The scoop of vanilla ice cream slid off his pie.

That night, Glenn and Karen slept back to back, careful not to touch.

At breakfast, Karen said, "Since you won't go with me to a show, I'll go with you to your Club. At least we'll be together."

Annoyed, Glenn said, "We're together six nights a week." As a single man, he had spent six nights a week at the Club.

"What's your point?"

"Even God rested on the seventh."

"Being with me wears you out, is that it?" She folded her arms across her chest and added, "And since when are you so eager to live like God?"

Glenn changed his approach. "Karen, you'd be bored stiff at the Club. It's just a bunch of guys who play with trains." Had someone described his Club this way to him, his face would have taken on the red glow of a signal lantern, his ears would have chugged steam, and the person who had made the remark would have been run over without a warning whistle. Glenn had worked his way through college as a brakeman for Burlington Northern and knew all the rules of railroad safety, the exact rivet design on most tenders, the brake rigging and air-hose design of each locomotive, and how to reduce and design a building to perfect H.O. scale and build it from scratch. Railroaders from clubs as far away as Kenosha and Madison came by to see his brewery, grain elevator, and slaughterhouse and praised them as masterpieces of detail.

Determined, Karen added, "Cheryl goes with Bob sometimes, and I know for a fact she likes it."

"Ya, Bob's wife. She watches football and goes bowling and drinks more beer than he does. You're not like that." Karen thought, I guess it's just too much to ask, and gave up, which gave Glenn room to think, and whenever Glenn had plenty of room, he became generous in a way he could not be when he felt squeezed. At Thursday dinner, Glenn asked, "You still want to come with me tomorrow?"

On Friday evening, Glenn opened the door at the Great Northern Railroad Club, turned to his wife, and said, "Welcome."

"Thank you," she answered, walking by him. Once inside, she paused and let her husband take the lead. He walked alongside a rack of blue metal lockers and stopped so abruptly that she walked into his backside. Glenn turned his head and looked at Karen. "Well I'm sorry!" she said. "I didn't know you were going to stop on a dime."

Glenn opened his locker, took out a blue-and-gray striped cap and tucked his black bangs under the cap, which highlighted his tall, pale, oily forehead. He pulled out a matching striped apron, put the top strap over his head, and spread the apron across his big stomach. Karen stepped behind him and cinched the apron strings before tying them. "Not so tight," he complained. "I'd like a little blood to get to my legs." She loosened the strings and tied them in a double bow. "Come on," he said, "I'll give you a tour."

The railroad layout was built in the center of the warehouse, an H.O. continent. Huge pipes and vents, painted blue and white, crisscrossed the ceiling above the layout. The couple stood next to Mt. Brillion, a handpainted papermaché mountain reinforced with chicken wire and named after James Brillion, founder and Trainmaster of the Great Northern Railroad Club. Groves of tiny fir trees covered Mt. Brillion's lower slopes and white sand from Lido Beach, Florida, was sprinkled on the slopes above timberline. A black locomotive pulled five cars loaded with lumber into the Mt. Brillion tunnel, reappeared on the other side of the mountain, and circled Bluegill Lake. Two men with fishing poles sat in a green rowboat in the lake.

Glenn walked alongside a collection of tiny buildings, pointed, and said, "That's our town, Four Corners." Karen walked behind him, studying the town. People with shopping bags strolled the sidewalks and visited with one another on street corners. A black-and-white dog, its rear leg lifted, stood next to a red fire hydrant. Karen thought, only a man would think of that. Without warning, the building lights dimmed until the tiny streetlights and railroad signals stood out brightly. Ceiling lights flashed on and off. Karen flinched. A boom and rattle followed, as if someone was pounding on the ceiling pipes with a stick. Glenn said, "That's our thunderstorm. Every hour on the hour." The railroad layout made Karen remember with pleasure the days she had created a miniature world with dolls and dollhouses.

She startled Glenn by asking, "Can I run a train?"

"Well, no. Only members can," he said. "But you can watch me." He walked alongside the railroad yard and looked at the lineup of trains. She followed him up four stairs and onto the raised engineer's deck. Glenn sat down in a vacant engineer's seat and Karen sat next to him in another seat, in line with four other engineers. Glenn put on the headmike and spoke through it to a heavy, white-haired man seated in a windowed booth. "Dispatch – this is Engineer Schneider requesting Westbound Main out of the Yard." Glenn pointed and said to Karen, "That's my Berkshire Steam Engine pulling ten hoppers of coal." The coal drag pulled out of the yard and onto Westbound Main, and Glenn forgot about Karen, his job, and his debts – it was just him, his brakeman, his conductor, and four-hundred tons of coal riding the rails.

Feeling ignored, Karen began talking to Bob, who sat to her right. She asked, "Where's Cheryl tonight?"

"At her Mom's."

"I wish I could run a train," Karen added.

"You do? Well, you can run one of mine, just for a minute." Bob talked to the dispatcher and received clearance for his train on Westbound Main. Leaning toward Karen, he explained the control panel to her, pointed at the layout, and asked, "See that Wabash covered wagon?" She nodded. "You're pulling a steam-generator car and the Wabash President's private car. She's all yours." Karen guided her train out of the yard and between the grain elevator and slaughterhouse. Bob said, "Easy does it," but by the time her train disappeared into the Mt. Brillion tunnel, the Wabash President was really moving.

Karen put her eye on the other end of the tunnel, waiting for her train to appear. She blinked three times when a slow-moving coal drag chugged out of the tunnel. That's not my train, she thought. Where's my train? She glanced at Bob just as her train roared out of the tunnel and crashed into the red caboose of the coal drag. The caboose and several coal-hoppers fell off the tracks and onto their sides, spilling tiny chunks of coal into Bluegill Lake. The Wabash President, who had been standing on the rear porch of his car, was thrown into the lake and landed face down near the green rowboat.

Glenn pounded his control panel with his fist and Karen jumped. He stood and glared at the row of engineers. "Who ran that covered wagon up my rear end?" he yelled. The men looked at Glenn and shrugged, bewildered.

The dispatcher spoke through his headphones, "Look closer to home." Glenn looked down at Karen and saw that she wore a headset and a look which said, I'm afraid I'm the one who ran up your rear end, dear. He stared at her as if he had found her in bed with another man.

She whispered, "Glenn, sit down, you're embarrassing me."

"*I'm* embarrassing *you?*" he yelled.

Bob added, "It was my fault, Glenn. I set her up."

Not knowing what to say or do next, Glenn waved his hand in disgust and walked off the engineer's deck with deliberate strides, past his locker, and out the front door – still wearing his apron, cap, and headmike, muttering to himself in a way which was clear only to the dispatcher. Karen watched the door close behind her husband. "He walked out on me," she said, hurt. Three men in yellow hard-hats converged on the wreck. They pointed and talked in hushed voices, one man taking notes on a yellow pad of legal paper, another man aiming and flashing a Polaroid camera.

Karen looked at Bob and asked, "What are they doing?"

"That's our safety team," he said. "They have to inspect the accident and make a report at our Sunday night meeting. The Trainmaster will decide if any fines are in order."

"Fines?" Karen said, her hurt giving way to anger. "They're only toy trains! I ran into a toy train by accident – what're they going to do, put me in a toy jail?"

Bob said, "Just calm down, Karen."

"I want to go home."

"I'll take you."

Bob pulled up behind Glenn's white Impala. The house was dark and quiet, as if no one was home. The headlights from Bob's car gave light to Karen as she unlocked the front door. Once in the entry, she paused. Bob's headlights lit up the living room as he backed out of the driveway, and she saw Glenn lying on the couch under a blanket, his back to her. Karen had not slept apart from Glenn since their wedding nine months earlier, but then she had never been in a train wreck with him or fought with him in front of his friends. Without speaking, she walked to their bedroom, undressed, and got in bed, though she could not sleep.

Glenn got up from the couch and walked down the dark hall, running his fingers along each wall to guide him to the bedroom. He stopped at the door and looked into the dark room. Karen held her breath, waiting to hear him speak, but he said nothing, turned, and walked back to the living room.

The next morning, Glenn began to hang the storm windows without Karen, but he found it awkward to work without her and badly pinched both thumbs. Soon, he retreated to his basement workbench and switched on the radio, turning the dial until he heard a woman author talking about her newest book, *How To Keep Love Alive*. He listened to her as he began designing a new model for the railroad layout, a house for Four Corners. Upstairs, Karen set up a card table in front of the television and pieced together a thousand-piece puzzle of a castle on the Rhine River. She phoned Cheryl, told her about the train wreck, and asked, "Do you and Bob ever fight?"

Cheryl said, "I'm like a cat, he's like a dog. When he gets mad, he chases me up a tree, and I wait up there until he stops barking. Then I come down and we talk."

"I don't know how to hiss or bark. I just worry."

"If you want to worry, worry about what you're going to say at tomorrow night's business meeting at the Club. Mr. 'Mt. Brillion' himself will rule on your accident."

"I'm not going."

"The men will lose respect for you."

"I don't care what those turds think of me."

"Then go for yourself."

Glenn and Karen ate dinner together, but they did not talk. He slept on the couch, again. Neither knew how to start over.

Sunday was like Saturday. After a silent dinner, Glenn got in his Impala and drove to the business meeting at the Club. Folding chairs had been arranged in rows which faced the scene of the accident. The front two rows were filled with Great Northern members. Glenn sat on a chair in the back row, by himself. James Brillion sat behind a card table at the front of the assembly. He stood and pounded a gavel on a block of walnut. "As duly elected Trainmaster of the Great Northern Railroad Club, I call this business meeting to order." His voice was deep and loud, full of the moral authority he had gained from forty years as a foreman at Cutler & Hammer. The men quieted and the front door opened. A blast of cold air curled around the men like a snake, and they all turned their heads. Karen and Cheryl stood in the doorway. Karen bit her lip.

Cheryl whispered, "You got what it takes for this." Without taking off their coats, the women sat at the other end of the back row, leaving seven empty chairs between them and Glenn.

"First order of business is the accident report," said the Trainmaster. "I've studied the written report and the photos. Frank is the Safety Foreman."

Frank stood, walked up to the layout, and reconstructed the events leading up to the accident. He pointed to the scene of the wreck with an extended locomotive antenna and ended his report by saying, "It weren't a pretty sight."

The Trainmaster said, "It's my job to rule on this accident. First, I got to fine myself. I was dispatcher the night of the wreck and I put two trains – one loaded and one light – on Westbound Main, too close together. Ten dollar fine." Gavel. The Trainmaster looked at Bob. Bob took off his cap and stood. "You helped a non-member run a train. Ten dollar fine." Bob nodded and sat. Gavel. The Trainmaster looked at Glenn.

Glenn stood, laid his arms across his stomach, and folded his hands in front of his groin. The Trainmaster said, "You did nothing wrong – until you fled the scene of the accident. Ten bucks." The gavel sounded and Glenn dropped into his chair.

The Trainmaster looked at Karen, and she stood. "You ran a train?"

"Yes." The men leaned into one another, murmuring, and Karen worried that her knees might give out from under her.

"You knew this was against our rules?"

"Yes."

"You were in the wrong. But I can't fine a non-member."

Cheryl stood and asked, "May I have a moment with my client?" The trainmaster nodded. Cheryl turned to Karen. "You want to snub these turds or do you want to get your foot in their door?" Karen whispered, "I want in." Counsel was given and received, and Karen announced, "I will accept a fine."

The Trainmaster lit a cigarette and studied Karen. The silver percolator sighed and bubbled behind him. "Very well," he said. "Dust our layout once a week for the next month with that special feather duster over there." Karen nodded and sat. The Trainmaster pounded his gavel three times and said, "Let's hear the treasurer's report."

After the meeting, Karen began to pay off her fine, dusting the top of Mt. Brillion and working her way toward lower elevations. Several men folded up chairs and others gathered around the silver percolator, pouring coffee, talking. Glenn, with his back to Karen, spoke to Bob, who apologized again. Glenn said, "Don't worry about it."

Cheryl stood by Karen at the far end of the layout as she dusted Glenn's slaughterhouse and grain elevator at the edge of Four Corners and said, "Your husband built most of the buildings, you know."

"I know," Karen said. Karen began dusting the residential section of Four Corners but paused and asked Cheryl, "This limestone house with the pink trim and gray shingles – has it been here long?"

Cheryl looked at the house. "Never seen it till this minute – must be new."

Karen leaned toward the new house and noticed a bird bath in front of the house and a large oak tree in the back yard. A man and woman stood on the front porch, holding one another like ballroom dancers, dressed in tuxedo and gown. "Oh!" Karen said to Cheryl. "That's our house! That's me and him on the front porch, dancing. We haven't danced since the day of our wedding!" Karen realized that Glenn had spent the last few days in his workshop, building this model of their house for Four Corners. She turned and looked at her husband, and at that moment, as if he felt her gaze, he turned away from Bob and looked at her.

LAZY IKE

HIS LITTLE HANDS lay in his lap, trembling with pleasure, and I wanted to touch them, not to stop them from trembling, but so that my hands might tremble with his. He sat across from our bush pilot and kept an eye on the instrument panel and the wild blue yonder ahead. When we flew into our first cloud, he pushed against the back of his seat and closed his eyes, expecting a crash. No crash. He opened his eyes and watched the prop chop up the cloud and spray its white blood against the windshield.

The sweep of lakes below us looked like seeds that had once been scattered from the sky, taken root in the granite and grown dark and bottomless, pushing back the forest. I turned to the vacant seat next to me. "Remember our first trip, Dad?" I asked, as if he were alive and looking at me. Dad took me on my first fishing trip to Canada when I was the age of my son, ten. We didn't fly. We drove to the end of the road, to Bigstone Lodge on Lake of the Woods, an Ontario lake the size of Rhode Island.

The pilot banked hard to the left – interrupting my memory – and pointed to a long, narrow lake below us. He brought the Beaver into the wind, set her down on the lake, and taxied toward shore. After killing the engine, he opened the door, stepped onto a float, and guided the plane along a log dock with his tall, leather boot. Bryan and I stepped onto the dock and looked at the log cabin set back in the pines, a set of moose antlers above the door like an address sign. Bryan pointed and asked the pilot, "They got moose here?"

"Keep an eye out, you'll see one this week."

The pilot got back in the plane and handed us our gear – sleeping bags; a cooler full of apples, oranges, and milk; a box of canned goods labeled in French and English; rod case; khaki duffle bags; and the blue plastic tackle box which weighed as much as Bryan. Driven by the fear that if we ran out of fishing tackle in the bush we were not to be forgiven, I had bought spinners and spoons, divers and floaters, plugs and poppers – brought to my senses by a conversation with a sales clerk at Jim's Sport Heaven. I had asked him, "Does this fluorescent orange attract northerns?"

"I'm not sure," he replied. "But I know it attracts fishermen."

The pilot climbed into his seat, put on his earphones, looked down on us, and hollered, "See you on Friday, about noon. There are planes flying every day so if you got an emergency, shoot up a flare." He looked at Bryan. "Take care of your Daddy. Let him catch the biggest fish."

Bryan must have fancied him a sort of military figure because he saluted him and said, "Yes sir!"

The plane roared down the lake and was soon just a speck over the trees. The buzz of the engine gave way to a silence that dropped on us from above like an invisible mist. I put my finger to my lips and curled my hand around my ear.

Bryan looked around, listening. "What are we listening to?"

"The quiet," I whispered.

He raised his blond eyebrows. "Oh."

"The quiet up here is so old if it had a face it would have wrinkles as deep as this lake."

"Is it a kind face, Dad?" His question made me do a lot of thinking, especially with the way the trip turned out.

The cabin was no-nonsense northwoods: log walls, plywood floor, one big room, three small windows, several bunks in one corner near a woodstove. As a courtesy to 20th-century fishermen and moose hunters who couldn't face life without appliances, there was a white porcelain refrigerator and propane stove. Bryan said, "That's my bunk," and we unrolled our sleeping bags, put away our supplies, and assembled our rods and reels.

We went out the back door and followed a trail to the outhouse, a hundred steps behind the cabin. I held open the door, and Bryan walked in, looked down, and said "P.U!" The underground mountain of fisherman poop came to a peak within three feet of the stool hole. "What do they do when it gets filled up?" he asked.

"Dig another hole and move the outhouse."

"Think you and I can fill it up?"

"We'll do our best."

We walked through the pines which surrounded the cabin. Pine sap glistened in the sun and smelled as sweet as acid. Turning around, I looked for the cabin, already hidden by the trees. I knelt in front of Bryan and held him by the shoulders. "Don't ever get out of sight of our cabin if you're not with me. And don't ever go near the lake without me, you understand?" He saluted.

At the lake, we climbed onto a shoreline boulder the size of our cabin, took off our sneakers and socks, sat down and splashed our pale, bony feet in the dark, cold water. I pulled a blue notebook – which I had found on our cabin table – out of my back pocket. On the cover: *Skinny Lake Fisherman's Log.*

I flipped pages full of ballpoint scribbling until I found the last entry and read from the page: "*Captain's Log, Stardate Aug. 2. Caught only one walleye before we had to pack up this morning, but we did catch two mice in the traps last night and boy were they good eating.*"

Bryan's little shoulders bounced with laughter, which carried across the lake, hit the other shore, and came back. "Keep reading!" he said.

"*Captain's Log Supplemental. It is now 9:32 a.m., and the plane isn't here. Are we going to be here forever? I hope not, because the beer is gone. It is now 9:37. One person has just died due to lack of beer. I don't know how we can hold out. It is 9:50 now, and we just sent the dead person out into the lake in a burning boat – ah, the plane.*"

We both laughed, and I stood. "What are we waiting for? Let's go fishing!"

I cut the ten-horse Evinrude near an underwater rock shelf which plunged toward hell. A patch of water lilies grew on the shelf, and I knew that a northern pike lived in those lilies, just like I knew that far below the reach of sunlight and fishing lures, at the bottom of that rock shelf, there lived a pike bigger than our boat, gorging himself on chubs since the last Ice Age.

I opened my tackle box, saw Dad's Lazy Ike, and thought

again of my first trip to Canada. The wind came up one afternoon while Dad and I were drifting for walleyes in big water. Dad studied the lake. Rough water scared him, and he obeyed a saying he had learned from his father, "Whitecaps on the lake – get to shore for God's sake!" He must have seen a whitecap, because he rolled his eyes so that the whites flashed like the foaming crest of a wave, and he motored us around a point and into a sheltered cove.

As soon as he killed the motor, I let fly with a cast alongside a birch which had fallen into the lake. "I got one!" I yelled. My rod tip bobbed and dipped. Dad netted the thrashing smallmouth, put it on a stringer, returned it to the lake and looked at my lure in the net, a plastic, orange flatfish.

"That smallie hit this?" he asked, astonished. Dad used only one lure for casting, a wooden, red-headed, white-bodied lure called Lazy Ike. He'd say, "It's like waving a red cape in front of a bull. Fish can't resist! The white gives it that flash in the sun and helps it stand out in dark water." He looked at me, his face showing pride and kindness – one of the last times I can remember him looking at me without fear or anger etched in his face like wrinkles, without whiskey on his breath. I left home at eighteen and didn't care to see him much after that. He died when Bryan was three.

Bryan interrupted my memory. "Give me that lure."

I handed him the Lazy Ike. "That's your grandpa's lure. Look at the teeth marks all over it." Bryan studied the lure for a moment, hooked it to his leader, and let fly with his first Canadian cast.

The Ike plopped on the water near the lilies, floated motionless for a second, then began its fierce wiggling dive. A moment later, Bryan's rod tip jerked and a pike's long white belly flashed in the sun as it tried to twist away from that Lazy Ike. "I got one, Dad!" The pike spit the hooks, the line went limp, and Bryan looked at me in the same way he had looked at me after striking out during the little league playoffs last spring, astonished such a defeat could happen in life.

We fished the shorelines for several hours and caught a dozen pike, which we called "stink bombs" because of their protective coat of smelly slime. Each time we grabbed the writhing body in the net, we got "slimed." By late afternoon I realized that Dad wasn't going to pass out any peanut butter sandwiches on this trip, so I motored us to a small rock-and-pine island, built a fire, and filleted two small northerns while Bryan watched. "You do the last one," I said. He gripped the slippery body and slowly worked the blade through the green and white scales and into the white flesh. His tongue curled around his upper lip as if it was helping him guide the knife.

Bryan was so tired that evening that he fell asleep on top of his sleeping bag before dark. I unzipped his bag and stuffed him in, arm by arm and leg by leg, without waking him. I poured myself a glass of brandy, put on my heavy sweater and went to sit on that shoreline boulder. The granite still held heat from the afternoon sun, and I wondered if it stored light as well as heat and might glow at night. The loons began their lonesome warbling, calling not to each other but to that silence, the silence with a kind face. I wanted to stay up and see the stars but I too was tired, so I closed up the cabin and was soon asleep on the bunk next to my son.

Late that night, I heard his voice in my ear, "Dad, I got to go pee," so I got my flashlight and took him to the outhouse.

We found a daily routine – breakfast at the cabin, fishing, shoreline lunch, fishing, dinner back at the cabin. Each evening we added an entry in the log book: *Stardate, August 4th. Took a dozen walleyes from our honey hole next to big rock island. Walleyes were black and gold, beautiful. We almost have enough walleye cheeks for a gourmet meal.* Bryan learned to clean fish, run the outboard, and get comfortable with the outhouse.

On our last evening, I drank the rest of my brandy while Bryan cast from the shoreline boulder with Dad's Lazy Ike. He hung it up in the branches of a birch which arched over the water, and we could not shake it loose. He threw sticks and rocks at the Lazy Ike in hopes of knocking it out of the tree, but soon it was dark, and I cut his line. He looked up at me. I said nothing but was disgusted that he lost Dad's Ike. "I'm sorry," he said, looking down. I wonder now what he saw in my face.

I woke up in darkness and felt a cool breeze on my face, so I fumbled for the flashlight on the floor, switched it on and saw the open back door. I jerked the light to Bryan's bunk – his sleeping bag was thrown open and empty. I called out, "Bryan!" and flashed the light around the cabin. "Bryan!" I jerked myself out of my sleeping bag, pulled on my pants and sweater, and lit the propane lantern above the stove. I ran out the door in my bare feet, yelling toward the lake, "Bryyyyan!" Nothing. I thought, this must be a dream, please God, this must be a dream! Where can he be?

I ran down the path to the lake, tripped on a root and broke my big toe, though I didn't know it then. The boat was next to the dock. I climbed onto the boulder and shouted at the top of my lungs, "Bryyyyyaaaan!" My voice carried out into the lake to the other shore and came back. When I heard that echo of my own voice hollering for my son, I shuddered and my blood went cold. I ran up and down the lake shore until I lost my breath, hoping to God that I wouldn't see his body floating in the water. I thought, now sit down and figure this out. Where could he be? Did he get up to look for that Lazy Ike? To go pee? Jesus, what time is it anyway?

The next couple of hours were a blur. I yelled until I was hoarse. Barefoot, I ran in larger and larger circles around the cabin. I got in the boat and rowed up and down the shore, yelling, listening for his voice. Once back at the cabin, I found the flare gun, ran to the shoreline boulder, and shot a flare into the night sky over the lake. The flare whistled, popped, burst into an orange ball of light, dropped, hit the black water, and sank, still glowing. The northern lights glowed across the night sky, fluttering like a curtain which separates this world from the next. "God, how beautiful!" I said. The next few hours are a blackout for me.

I sat on the shoreline boulder, watched the sky go from black to blue, and began to feel my body again – swollen toe, scratches across my face, a weariness so heavy that I worried about passing out. I had no idea where to look for my son or whether he was alive or dead, but I kept him alive in my mind's eye, lost in the woods somewhere, waiting for me to find him. Our plane was due at noon.

As the sun rose behind the trees on the opposite shore, I caught a movement out of the corner of my eye. Dad! He sat on the other side of the boulder, watching the sun. His black wavy hair is just as I remember it, I thought. But his face, oh, his face, how it's changed! No fear. No anger. No strain – as open as a clearing in the forest! He wore his fishing shirt, a blue, green, and red plaid Pendleton which he had loved so much we buried him in it. As soon as he turned his face toward me, my body let down, my shoulders dropped, and I sobbed until my hands were covered with snot. I looked up, figuring he'd be gone, but he was still there.

"Is Bryan alright?" I asked.

"Yes." It was as if I was hearing his voice for the first time, manly, beautiful, full of care yet without a care in the world.

"Can you tell me how to find him?"

"Yes."

Later that morning, just before the float plane circled our cabin and landed on our lake, I added a final entry into the fisherman's log. My hand trembled as I wrote:

Captain's Log, Stardate August 11th. Youngest crew member got up at night and in direct violation of captain's orders tried to find the outhouse without his flashlight and without escort. Got lost in woods. Search and Rescue efforts failed. Captain damn near went berserk. Help arrived from another world. Found youngest crew member – cold and scared, but unhurt – on second ridge behind cabin. Lost red-and-white Lazy Ike high in birch tree by shoreline boulder. Fish can't resist it! The red is like waving a cape in front of a bull. The white gives it that flash in the sun and helps it stand out in dark water.

If you can get it down, it's yours.

LIVE NATIVITY

"**W**HY SHOULD *your family* represent *The Holy Family?*" This final question on the application did not intimidate Ruth. She wrote, "Because we have what it takes to get the job done. I will sew the costumes. Don will get the animals. The kids will do their parts." In her mind, Ruth was already practicing the gestures and looks which would make her a memorable Virgin Mary.

Like so many elaborate traditions, the outdoor nativity at Immanuel Lutheran Church had humble origins. In 1949, when Ruth was ten, the congregation honored Rudolf Blau for fifty years of service as a trustee. His gift: an electric jigsaw. His first jigsaw project: life-size plywood cutouts of a cow, donkey, angel, and of course, a man, woman, and child in a manger. On the Saturday before Christmas, Rudolf pitched his canvas wall tent on the church's front lawn, tied open the front flaps, and arranged his cutouts in and around the tent. Thinking of the long winter nights, he illuminated the nativity with red and green spots, a "round the clock witness" to everyone who passed by.

Each year, Rudolf re-created the outdoor nativity, and

each year he added a new cutout: another angel, shepherd, or palm tree. After Rudolf's death in 1956, the congregation upgraded the tradition, replacing Rudolf's cutouts with live animals and real people, a live nativity. A real baby was used to represent Jesus until Evelyn Kolander's three-month-old, Carl, frostbit his ears and almost lost his lobes. After that, a handsome doll – donated by Evelyn – was used to represent Jesus.

Success brought trouble, as it always does. People began to maneuver for the chance to represent the Holy Family. Once, two Holy Families – in full costume – arrived at the nativity and argued bitterly for space inside the stable, one shepherd even raising his staff in a threatening way. When Pastor Schultz heard this, he had moved quickly to restore moral order, chartering a Nativity Council with full authority for choosing one Holy Family each year. The charter had created an application process which read in part: "Seeking God's will, all Council decisions will be made by secret vote and must be unanimous."

On the first of November, the Council, four retired men who had worked their way up through the ranks of the usher core met in Pastor Schultz's darkly paneled office. Each had reviewed the forty-six applications. Without any discussion, Pastor Schultz said, "Gentlemen. May I have your first ballots, please." The men put their ballots face down on his mahogany desk. Pastor Schultz adjusted the knot on his necktie, a little gesture he used whenever he needed a moment to think before speaking or acting. Last year, he had supervised eight ballots and seven arguments before unanimity and had gotten home after midnight. Pastor Schultz picked up the ballots like a poker player might pick his hand off the table, deliberately, one ballot at a time. His face showed nothing until he picked up the last ballot and lifted his eyebrows like he had been dealt four aces. "It's the Lord's doing," he said. "Unanimous on the first ballot." He picked up the receiver on his black phone and dialed Ruth's number.

Her eyes filled with tears when she heard his voice. "I had faith," she said. "The Council won't be sorry they chose us."

That next morning, Don stood in front of the steamed mirror, naked, except for the shower towel wrapped around his waist. He lathered his cheeks and chin with shaving cream and lifted the razor to his face just as Ruth came into the bathroom. "Wait!" she shouted. Don froze. She took the razor out of his hand and said, "I'll give you this back after the live nativity." For the next fifty-six days, Don grew his beard and Ruth prepared herself and her family for the first century A.D.

On the Saturday before Christmas, Ruth, still in bed, listened to her transistor radio. Her favorite deejay from Sheboygan, Early Bird Bob, said, "Cold today. High of twenty. Chance of snow by evening."

Ruth threw back the quilt. "It's going to be cold in Bethlehem tonight! I better get out the warmest stuff we've got." At noon, she looked at the thermometer outside the dining room window. "Come on, sweetie, you can do better than that!"

After lunch, Don drove to the church. Four men in heavy parkas, the Nativity Council members, stood next to a pile of barn boards and two-by-fours on the church's frozen front-lawn. The limestone church building behind them looked like a castle rising above the planted pines and spruce. Two hours later, the men dropped their hammers onto the ground and stood back to admire the stable, a three-walled shed which looked like a large chicken coop, the open wall facing Main Street. Don built a three-rail corral alongside the stable. His 4-H friends had assured him that by evening the corral would be filled with blue-ribbon stock.

When Don got home, he found the nativity equipment laid out on the front room couch: mittens, socks, scarves, parkas, and Ruth's carefully tailored costumes. Ruth thought, thank God I made the costumes roomy enough to fit over heavy clothes. At dusk, Don put on his felt-lined Sorel boots and electric socks and yelled, "Time to go!"

Ruth wasn't ready. She looked at him crossly and said, "Don't rush me! This is a once-in-a-lifetime experience. I want to enjoy every minute of it." Once she got her children, Wayne and Leslie, into the back seat, she got in the front seat next to Don and said, "Let's drive by slowly so we see how it all looks from the street." Don slowed by the nativity and each of them studied the scene. Ruth noticed a long, shaggy neck rising above the rails of the corral like a periscope. She pointed and shouted, "What's that?"

Don said, "Oh, that's Walt's llama. Ain't he a beaut?"

Ruth put her hands over her face and sobbed. Don pulled over to the curb and parked. "Well, now what's the matter?" he asked. In between sobs, she said, "… There were no llamas … at Bethlehem…. it looks like … like a …"

Wayne said, "Like a giraffe!"

Don flashed him a "Shut up this instant!" look through the rear-view mirror and touched his wife's knee. "Now look, Ruthy," he said. "There must have been a camel or two at the stable in Bethlehem, right?" She stopped sobbing and parted her fingers so that she could look at his face. "That llama looks like a small camel to me," he added, smiling.

"You really think so?" she said, so reassured by this thought that she let her hands slide down her face and into her lap. She looked again at the llama, tilting her head for a fresh angle on the whole scene.

Don parked in the parking lot next to the Fireside Room and Pastor Schultz opened the door. Behind him, a four-log fire crackled and hissed in the stone fireplace. Each family member brought in their own folded costume and sat on the large couch, facing the fire and a wooden box which rested on the hearth. The box was handpainted with midnight blue enamel and dozens, perhaps hundreds, of tiny, white stars. Pastor Schultz removed the box lid, lifted out a large doll swaddled in a blanket, and handed the doll to Ruth as if he were handing her a newborn. Ruth took the doll tenderly and folded back the swaddling clothes from around its face. "Oh," she said. "How lovely he is." Don leaned over to see the doll's face. It was an old doll with a white porcelain head, rosy cheeks, dark hair, and bright blue eyes. Don thought that the doll looked a lot more like a girl than a boy, but since Ruth seemed to accept the doll without question, he said nothing. Each Holy Family had used this doll since the case of infant frostbite.

Pastor Schultz adjusted the knot on his tie and said, "It's nearly time for you to dress. Let us pray." He bowed his head, and the others did the same. "Dear Holy Father. We pray that all of us here may know the joy and terror of the Holy Family." Ruth flinched when he used the word, terror. As the mother of two pre-teens, she thought that plenty of terror made its way into her life without an explicit invitation.

Ruth supervised her family as they dressed. "Layers," she said. "Get dressed in layers." Wayne pulled his brown shepherd's robe over his head, wiggled it down his parka, and walked to a full-length mirror mounted on the wall and most often used by Lutheran brides.

Disgusted, he said, "It looks like a bathrobe." Ruth ignored his comment and pinned gold-painted plastic wings to the back of Leslie's white angel robe. Don buttoned up his beige peasant's robe over his blaze-orange deer hunting coveralls. The robe perfectly hid the gaudy coveralls but ended halfway down his Sorel boots, so the first and twentieth centuries collided visibly just above his ankles. Ruth raised her own arms and let the Marion-blue robe fall around her body. She picked up the doll and walked to the mirror. Seeing herself as the Virgin Mary, she thought back to that day, fourteen years earlier, when she had stepped in front of that mirror as a virgin bride just before her wedding ceremony. Slowly, she pulled the blue hood over her head like she had once pulled the bridal veil over her face. No one rushed her.

Don led the procession out of the Fireside Room and into the cold like Joseph must have once led his family into the dark streets of Bethlehem. The family walked single-file behind him, silently, around the corner of the church. A brilliant floodlight hung over the front of the stable from a wire strung between two spruce trees. The family walked alongside the corral, which held a black-faced ram, a gray Shetland pony, a pygmy goat, a tiny burro, and the llama, which looked at Ruth. She looked away.

Don led his wife, the babe in her arms, to the wooden

manger inside the stable. He bent down, gathered an armful of straw from the thick straw floor and lined the manger. Ruth laid the baby Jesus on the bed of manger straw and stepped behind the manger with Don, facing the street.

Leslie asked, "Can we talk?"

Ruth answered, "Only if you must."

A car came down Main Street, slowed, and honked. Don waved.

"Don't go waving to every Tom, Dick, and Harry," Ruth said.

"That wasn't Tom, Dick, or Harry. That was Fred and Olga."

Wayne pulled his shepherd's hood over his forehead and said to Leslie, "I hope none of my friends drive by." Other cars drove by. Most stopped, and a line of cars began to form in front of the live nativity.

It was so cold that most people did not get out of their cars, but one man got out of his car and walked up to the stable. He studied the silent Holy Family and the animals in the corral. "I never read about no llama being in Bethlehem," he said.

Ruth said, "Well now Mr. Fenster, how would you know? You Catholics don't read your bibles anyway!"

Leslie got cold first. "My feet are cold, Mom."

Ruth looked at her daughter. "Wiggle your toes. Massage your ear lobes."

Don added, "Why don't you flutter around a little. God gave you wings."

Leslie walked to the manger, looked at the doll, and said, "It's a girl, Mom."

Ruth said, "No, dear. It's a boy."

Don whispered to Ruth, " I think it looks a lot like a girl too, those rosy cheeks and all."

Ruth turned to her husband and asked with contempt, "Where's your faith?" Don bent over and turned on his electric socks.

The Holy Family faced another two hours in the cold. Leslie pressed her mittened hands against her cheeks. When Don saw snowflakes in the headlights of the parked cars, he said, "That's it! I'm going to get some wood from the Fireside Room and build a warming fire."

Ruth brought up a theological challenge. "Would Joseph have left the baby and done that?"

Irritated, he replied, "Joseph didn't have two other children to worry about now did he?"

Don walked across the frozen lawn into the darkness, returning with an armful of split oak and kindling. He knelt in front of the stable, cleared a bare spot in the straw and arranged the kindling like a tepee. Wayne and Leslie stood hard by as he struck the match.

At eight o'clock, the batteries in Don's socks went dead. The fire was nearly out too, one log still glowing. Don said, "I'm calling a hot chocolate break." Wayne and Leslie bolted toward the church.

Ruth looked at her husband. "How dare you let them run off?" She motioned her head toward the line of parked cars and asked, "What are those people to think?"

Don said, "They probably think we're freezing to death and they'd be right." He looked at the doll in the manger and added, "Let's take a break. Little girl Jesus can make it without us for a while."

"I'm staying right here by *his* side!" Ruth said. She folded her arms across her chest and planted her feet. "Fine, you stay," Don said. "I'll see to the kids." Ruth stood her vigil, alone, while the adults in the parked cars tried to explain to their children why the Holy Family seemed to be splitting up. Ten minutes later, Ruth walked off too, and all twelve cars pulled away from the curb together, like a caravan.

After ten minutes in front of the fire, Don said, "Let's start our second shift." He opened the outside door and stepped into the cold but fell back against the church wall when he heard pounding hooves coming at him from the left. The Shetland pony and llama galloped past him, neck and neck. Don yelled, "Wayne! Let's get 'em!" Ruth and Leslie ran the other way, around the corner of the church, and stopped – paralyzed. Flames whipped twenty feet into the night sky and roared like a terrible wind, the stable burning like the wick of a giant torch raised against the night.

Ruth yelled to Leslie, "Don't move!" and ran toward the burning stable. Her foot caught in her robe and she fell to her hands and knees, but she got up and ran again. Near the stable, she put her hand in front of her face to block the heat, took a deep breath, and ducked. She grabbed the babe and ran onto the lawn, where she tore off the smoking blanket and held the naked doll to her chest. At twenty feet, she could feel the heat of the flames on her face and hands.

Don ran to her. "Are you nuts, woman?" he yelled. With his huge boots, he stomped the smoking blanket at her feet. Passing cars pulled over to witness this startling turn in nativity tradition. Several men ran across the lawn and joined the Holy Family, including Frank Boetcher with his camera. The stable roof collapsed and crushed the manger.

That next morning, Don opened the front door. An inch of new snow had fallen during the night, a fine snow which covered the ground like powdered sugar. He picked up the Tri-County Record from the sidewalk and opened it on his way to their bedroom. Ruth lay on her back in bed, looking at the ceiling, blinking. Earlier, she had told Don, "I don't feel too well. I just might spent all day in bed." Don held the Record's front page in front of her. She squinted and said, "Oh dear." In Frank Boetcher's black-and-white photo, she and Don were silhouetted in front of the burning stable, looking a lot like Rudolf Blau's plywood cutouts.

Don said, "I'll read you the caption: *Saviour Saved. A stray spark from a warming fire turned the Live Nativity, a Kiel tradition for 34 years, into a raging inferno. Holy Family okay.... Llama still missing.*" Don frowned. "I wonder where that damn giraffe is hiding?" The doorbell rang and Don added, "That'll be the Pastor. He wants see how you are doing before he goes to church." Ruth pulled back the quilt and looked at the doll lying next to her.

Pastor Schultz, still in his gray wool overcoat, walked into the bedroom with the midnight-blue box under one arm. He stood at the end of the bed and asked, "Ruth. Are you alright?"

"Yes. But Jesus lost his eyelids, burned right off."

Pastor Schultz set the empty box next to Ruth and she put the doll in it. He said, "Don't be too concerned about that. Not many people know this, but a few years ago Martha and Dudley dropped him on the asphalt as they were heading for the nativity and his head shattered into a dozen pieces. They covered him with a lot of straw and no one noticed. This is his second head." He winked and smiled, which calmed her.

After their visit, he paused at her door, the starry, midnight-blue box with Jesus under his right arm. He adjusted his necktie knot with his left hand and asked quietly, "Ruth, was it beautiful?"

Startled, she asked him, "Was what beautiful?"

"The fire."

"No. It was terrible."

Pastor Schultz nodded and said, "I have come to see that what is terrible can be beautiful too."

He turned to leave but she said, "Pastor – that fire is burning inside me now, roaring. I can't put it out. It's burning away what little faith I have."

Pastor Schultz turned toward her, and she saw his eyes swell with tears. He startled her again by saying, "That fire inside you is burning away everything *but* your faith. Let it burn, Ruthy, let it burn."

HER WHOLE FACE SAID YES

THE TIP OF BEN'S NOSE touched the thick glass of the incubator window as he watched a tiny beak break out of a brown eggshell. "Yaah, little one," he said. "You're the first." By week's end, Ben could look through each of his incubator windows and see hundreds of dark-eyed, fluff-ball pheasant chicks standing among broken eggshells, chirping like a yard full of crickets.

Two weeks later, Ben, and his wife, Cora, boxed the chicks, and Ben delivered them – and his itemized bill – to the Rockville Sportsman's Club. The Club's caretaker asked Ben, "Can we count on you for next year's birds then?"

Ben shook his head. "This was our last hatch."

"You and Cora retiring?"

"Yaah. No money in hatching anymore. Might as well retire."

On the first of June, the Hatchery Owners Association newsletter ran Ben and Cora's ad: *Saturday Auction at B&C Hatchery. Everything must go.* The hatchery stood alongside their house, both buildings painted white with blue shutters and separated by a row of blue spruce taller than the Elkhart

Lake town flagpole. Ben had planted the spruce as seedlings the size of his thumb.

On auction day, cars and pickups clogged the gravel drive which circled the hatchery. People from as far away as Manitowoc inspected the equipment and incubators. Cora walked through the hatch room with both hands under a large, blue platter of her Spiced Coffee Cake. When she ran low, she hurried to her kitchen next door for more. Ben greeted friends and neighbors but also kept an eye on the auctioneer and an ear on the bids, wincing when a bid topped out beneath his hope.

After the auction, Ben and Cora took hands and walked slowly through the empty hatchery. Their footsteps echoed off the bare walls. Ben said, "Made almost four tausend dollars today."

"It's so empty, so quiet," whispered Cora. A mouse ran across the concrete floor, looking for cover.

"I did some figuring," Ben said. "We hatched forty tausend this year. Eight hundred tausend over the years since we began."

"Oh dear!"

"Remember our first hatch? Five tausend Rhode Island Reds for the Helmuth Brothers. Am I right, Cora?"

"I was three months pregnant, that's what I remember."

At dusk, Ben padlocked the blue hatchery door and took down the Chicks For Sale sign.

Since the hatchery had always closed for the winter, the cold months passed much the same as they always had for Ben and Cora, but by Easter, the retired couple had grown restless. On warm days, Cora walked to their front-room window, hoping to see a car pull into the driveway. Once, at dinner, she had put down her fork and said, "I miss our customers." When someone phoned with a hatch inquiry, Ben would say, "Sorry. Out of business," but he'd still calculate how much money he might have made on that hatch. Both missed caring for something small and precious.

By the first of May, the soil in Ben's vegetable garden crumbled in his hand, and with his spade, he turned over a long, narrow strip of dirt. He ended his work by grabbing a fistful of the moist, dark soil, holding it under his nose, closing his eyes, and breathing in deeply. That evening, Ben reviewed the sixty-six page catalog from Meuser Nursery in Pennsylvania and filled out an order for two thousand Morheim Spruce, the bluest spruce money could buy.

Ten days later, the seedlings arrived in twenty bundles, and Ben unwrapped the paper from around each like a mother unwraps a blanket from around her newborn. He put the tiny blue trees in buckets filled with rain water and spent two happy days planting them, one by one, working on his knees with a hand trowel so that he could be close to the spruce, talking to them like he used to do with his chicks. "Yaah. You're as blue as they come. You'll fetch a fine price one day." When he was done planting, he walked up and down the long rows of tender, blue trees, nodding with satisfaction. Cora watched him from the kitchen window and thought, a man of eighty who can plant tiny trees has got hope in his blood. A newly painted blue and white sign now hung near their driveway entrance: TRUE BLUE SPRUCE FOR SALE. Ben was back in business.

Ben and Cora's daughter, Martha, visited from California

in early May and marveled about her mother's African violets, which lined the sill of every east widow. "Mother," she said, "I sure didn't get your green thumb. Have you ever tried to sell any of your violets?" This casual question inspired Cora to think about a new business for herself.

After Martha flew back to California, Cora said, "Ben. I got to go to Sheboygan this week."

"Oh?"

Sensing his reluctance to make the thirty-mile trip, she added, "Well, it could wait. But we might lose out on some money."

"I'm ready when you are," he answered.

The next day, Ben drove Cora to the Violets Are Blue Flower Shop in Sheboygan where she bought a blue-purple called Fantasy Sparkle, a fierce pink called Hot Toddy, a dark pink called Bohemian Sunset, and a dark purple called Lilac Morn. On the drive home, she looked at Ben. "How do you spell exotic?"

"How would I know such a thing?" he replied, frowning.

Cora repotted her new violets in clay pots and fit them in between her other violets. That afternoon, she went in the basement and painted over the CHICKS FOR SALE sign with white paint, and when that was dry, she dipped a new brush into a quart of PurplePlus paint and printed: EXOTIC AFRICAN VIOLETS HERE. She asked Ben to hang her sign underneath his TRUE BLUE SPRUCE FOR SALE sign. Cora was back in business too. Ben hung her sign but something about the wording bothered him. "You make it sound like you're giving them violets away," he told her, which is exactly what she did if she liked a person, she'd say, "Here, take this Blue Excitement home since you love it so much." Ben, on the other hand, would get top dollar for his blue spruce even if his customer had once saved his life in the war.

One warm morning in late June, Cora stood at the kitchen sink, repotting her rootbound Royal Purple and listening to the radio announcer warn of an approaching cold front from the Dakotas. She looked out the window and cocked her head, as if listening to an unusual sound. The bare-root plant slipped between her bony fingers and dropped into the sink, her eyes rolled into the back of her head, and she slumped to the floor, her small, slender body motionless on the yellow linoleum. Ben came in from the garden, said, "Oh, Cora!" and fell to his knees beside her.

A young man dressed in a blue-green smock walked up to Ben in the hospital corridor. "Are you Mr. Halbach?" Ben nodded. "I'm Doctor Hein. Your wife's had a small stroke. She's paralyzed on much of her right side."

"Will she be okay?"

"She'll recover, yes. But it's too early to tell how full her recovery will be."

Ben got Cora a private room with an east-facing window, brought five of her favorite violets for the window sill, and visited her every day. She smiled at him, but only the left side of her mouth moved. He read to her from *Violet Care* and *Ladies Home Journal*, and the daily devotion from *The Upper Room*. On Cora's fourth day in the hospital, Ben read the devotion, which ended with a passage from the gospel of John: "Truly, truly, I say to you, when you were young, you girded yourself and walked where you would; but when you are old, you will stretch out your hands, and another will gird you and carry you where you do not wish to go." Ben closed the little magazine and looked out the window, past her violets, past the parking lot to the woods which rose like a dark wall at the edge of the hospital lawn.

Twelve days after her stroke, Ben brought Cora home. Before she left the hospital, she gave a violet to each nurse who had cared for her. Cora was thin and quiet. Her right eyelid still drooped, the right side of her mouth was still paralyzed, her speech was labored and slow, but she could walk with a cane and eat and dress herself. As soon as she got in her kitchen, she plunged her forefinger into the soil of the Royal Purple which she had been repotting when she had the stroke. Cora pulled her finger out, looked at the moist, black dirt clinging to it. "Thanks for taking care of them, my husband."

The doctor had told Ben that Cora could have more strokes which might leave her temporarily helpless, so he left home only when necessary. If he had to leave her alone, he would say, "I'll be back 'fore you know it." Cora rarely left home, except to visit the doctor or physical therapist. She lay on their front-room couch for much of each day, and Ben took over the housecleaning and cooking. She continued to show her violets to people who saw her purple-and-white sign and stopped. One day, a Milwaukee woman who reminded Cora of her daughter stopped, and Cora gave her the last Burgundy Bonanza, a plant with bronze leaves and magenta flowers.

On the first of August, Ben walked back to the house from their roadside mailbox, looking at each piece of mail. He stopped, opened a red envelope, and pulled out a stiff card, which read:

You Are Invited To
The Annual Gala Dance at the Veterans Hall
Live Music by String of Pearls
September 3rd, 8:00 p.m.
Door Prizes Of Course
Sponsored by the Hatchery Owners Association

Cora was reading her devotion in the front room when Ben entered. She motioned for him to sit down, but he walked up to her and stood by her. She said, "Here's the thought for the day: 'Let your yes be yes and your no be no.'" He put the invitation in her lap and she looked at the card.

"Will you go with me?" he asked.

"Ben, go on!"

"If you don't go with me I'll take Denise Vogel," he added, grinning. Denise was the blonde whom Ben had taken to this same Labor Day weekend dance forty-five years earlier. His friend, Emil Stoll, had taken Cora to that dance, but each man had happily left the dance with the other's partner. Emil had married Denise and died ten years later. Denise had married twice more and lost each husband, and Cora had once said to Ben, "You're lucky you married me. You'd be long dead by now if you had married her."

Frowning, Cora said, "In case you forgot, I had a stroke. I can hardly walk around this house let alone dance."

"We don't have to dance," Ben added. "We can just listen to the music and visit."

She looked at the invitation in her hands. For the first time since her stroke, she felt a tingling up and down the right side of her face. She pinched her right cheek hard and smiled. She said nothing, but she looked up at Ben and her whole face said yes.

On the morning of the dance, Cora looked at Ben across their formica kitchen table and said, "I can't do this. I should never have said yes." After breakfast, they tied on one another's aprons and stood at the sink, side by side. Cora washed the first dish and passed it to Ben. "My right leg is still bum. You want me to hop around the dance floor on one leg?" Ben took the dish, saying nothing. She handed him a white coffee cup. "I'll fall on my head if I try to dance." Ben stayed silent. Cora handed him a juice glass. "Fine. It'll be your fault."

After breakfast, Ben drove Cora to Louise's Style Shop, downtown. He helped her into the shop, which had three pink, padded chairs and three pink hairdryers the size of bushel baskets. Ben drove to Vic's Grocery and Bait Store and returned for her an hour later. On their way home, Cora said, "I'm not going tonight."

"Be a shame for people to miss your new permanent." Cora said nothing, but patted her hair with an open hand. "Them lavender streaks look nice," Ben added.

"They're tints, not streaks."

After dinner, Ben put on his forest-green suit and his favorite tie, the tie of a hatchery owner, sky blue, with a hand-painted pheasant flushing from cover on the widest part. Cora sat on their bed and looked at her clothes in the closet. She decided against her navy suit and put on her burgundy dress with heavy gold buttons.

Ben drove to Veterans Hall, a red brick building next to the fire station, just off Main Street, and the couple walked arm in arm into the building. The ceiling of the hall was criss-crossed with red and white crepe paper, the official colors of the Hatchery Owners Association. Cora looked at the dozen round tables near the stage around which happy hatchery owners and their families chatted so loudly that Cora said, "Just like walking into a henhouse." She turned to Ben. "Get me a glass of wine, please."

Remembering that her pill bottles read: Do not mix with alcohol, he said, "Now you know I can't do that."

"Now you know one glass of wine won't kill me." Ben turned away and returned with a glass of dark red port in each hand.

They sat down next to Frank and Myrtle Knopf, and Ben and Frank traded complaints about the hatchery business. "Can't make money anymore," Frank said. "You two got out just in time."

The String of Pearls musicians walked onto stage and began to tune their instruments. All eight men and one woman wore red sport coats, white shirts, black trousers and bow ties. The baritone saxophonist was a short, thin man, barely as tall as his curved neck sax. The bass player said, "Ah-one, ah-two, ah-one-two-three-four," and the band began to play "Chattanooga Choo-Choo."

Denise Vogel made her entrance at mid-song in a silver-fox wrap. She was trailed by a handsome man with hair the color of the fox. The couple sat down at the table next to Ben and Cora. Ben leaned toward Cora. "I guess she finally got over me."

"He better watch out," Cora answered. "If he marries her he'll be dead sooner than he thinks. Who is he anyway?"

Cora finished her port with one big swallow as the band began to play "Sentimental Journey." She held out her hand and lowered her chin like the women do in those silent movies, and quoted an Old Testament passage, "King David danced with all his might before the Lord!" Ben smiled, rose from his chair, took her hand, and helped her to her feet. He picked up her cane and offered it to her, but she waved it off, and with small, shuffling steps, she walked onto the dance floor. He put one arm around her bony waist and she draped one hand on his shoulder. They clasped their other hands and began to move just their hips to the music. Cora looked at her feet and began to move them too, and when she saw that they obeyed her, she looked up at her husband. Cora took her hand off his shoulder and untwisted his tie so that the pheasant flushed into the open space between them rather than against his stomach. The scent of their colognes met just above the flushing pheasant, his Brut surrendering to her Evening In Paris, and they looked at one another with the kind of tenderness which takes a lifetime to build, the kind of look which says, yes, I remember our first dance right here forty-five years ago. Yes, I remember our first fight. Yes, I remember when I first saw fear in your eyes, and love. When the song ended, Cora leaned forward and spoke into Ben's good ear, "I don't think Denise has nearly the figure I do, do you?"

"Ha! She looks like an old hen to me."

That next morning, Cora rested in bed while Ben prepared breakfast. She heard her husband open and close the refrigerator door, crack four eggshells against the lip of the mixing bowl, and whip the eggs with a fork. When the eggs began sizzling in the frying pan, Ben shouted, "Come and get it, girl!" She sat up on the edge of the bed and reached for her pale yellow robe.

At breakfast, Ben said, "King David should have seen you dance last night."

"Go on!" Cora said, blushing. "I'm stiff as a board this morning."

"You take it easy today."

"Got an order to fill," Cora said.

"Oh?"

"Louise wants a dozen pink violets for her hair shop, said she'd pay me three dollars apiece."

Ben raised his eyebrows and said, "Thirty-six dollars!" He sipped his coffee. "I got an order to fill too."

"Oh?"

"I'm giving fifty spruce to the Sportsman's Club. They said the pheasants need more winter cover."

"Did you say *giving*?"

"Yaah. No charge."

"My goodness!" Cora said. "Wait till King David hears about this."

WIND CHILL

On November 9th, 1940, *a severe and unexpected snow-storm swept across North Dakota, Minnesota, and western Wisconsin. More than one hundred people and thousands of livestock perished in what has come to be known as the Armistice Day Blizzard.*

Adeline Olsen stared at her coffee cup, which rested bottom up on her desk and seemed to be making noises. Leaning back in her chair, she looked at her twelve students and noticed that the older boys were snickering. "Why is my coffee cup upside down?" she asked, worried that the boys were up to something at her expense. No one spoke. She tilted the cup and lowered her head for a look underneath the cup. A twitching, whiskered nose poked out and Miss Olsen pulled up her head like a startled mare, but realizing that this was a test, she did not scream. The mouse dashed across her geography book, hit the far edge of her desk, leaped into air, and dropped to the wood plank floor. The girls screamed and lifted their feet, and the mouse darted underneath the desks until Jimmy Schnee, the only eighth grader and oldest student, raised his leg and stomped it dead with his torn leather boot.

Jimmy lifted his boot, picked up the limp carcass by the tail, held it high, and said proudly, "Got him!"

Furious, Adeline took her geography book and walked to his desk. She was twenty years old and five months out of Downer Teachers' College, but nothing in her schooling had prepared her for a student like Jimmy – his clothes smelled like dirt, his intelligence showed only in pranks and fights, and his eyes carried the sadness of a man. She had been taught that the word G-O-D stood for Good-Orderly-Discipline, and that a teacher was justified in doing whatever it took to make this kind of G-O-D rule the classroom, so Adeline swung her arm and clipped Jimmy across his cheek with the heavy book, knocking him out of his desk, startling herself and the other students. Jimmy touched his cheek with his hand, rose slowly to his feet, turned, and walked out the front door, head down, uncombed bangs falling across his face. She followed him onto the porch and watched him cross the school yard, her mind racing: He had it coming ... that dead snake under my desk, that live toad in my coat pocket, now this mouse ... he mocks me ... he's got to learn respect.... No-No-No-No! I was wrong to hit him. I just didn't know what else to do. I must learn another way. Jimmy walked past the girl's outhouse, stopped, raised his arm, aimed, and tossed the mouse through the small hole in the closed door.

Adeline turned away from Jimmy when she heard a car coming down the lane toward her District 90 Schoolhouse, a white frame building with one room, one door, two outhouses, six windows as tall as a man, a pot-bellied stove, woodshed, and porch, built and opened in 1936. Mr. Anderson, a school board member, parked his black Buick under the curled, purple leaves of the schoolyard oak and got out, looking at the sky. "Hello there!" Adeline shouted.

"Miss Olsen. I come to warn you."

"About what?"

"A bad storm's on the way. Send the children home right away."

Adeline looked up. A few gray clouds drifted across the sky, and a warm, faint breeze blew against her face. She asked, "Are you sure, Mr. Anderson?"

"The radio announcer was sure."

"Very well then."

"We'll get your load of coal soon – it's been so warm nobody's thought about coal." Though most of the leaves were down, Indian summer lived on, with green lawns, cattle at pasture, chickens scratching in barnyards, and each day near sixty degrees by noon. Adeline called it "perfect sweater weather."

"I seen that Schnee boy leaving school. He in trouble again?" Without waiting for Adeline's answer, he added, "He's got a chip on his shoulder cause he's dirt poor and knows it. I heared his baby sister sleeps in a bureau drawer." Had he not been the man who had signed her contract, she would have corrected his usage.

Mr. Anderson drove away and Adeline walked back into her school and stood in front of her desk, where she made her announcements and gave her assignments. The students quieted. "Mr. Anderson just stopped by to let me know that a dangerous storm is on the way and I must let out school early."

Roger Schwartz, the second oldest boy after Jimmy, asked,

"When is early, Miss Olsen?"

"Now. I want you to collect your books and belongings and walk straight home – no dillydallying along the way. Have I made myself clear?" The children nodded and jumped out of their desks, happy that school was suddenly over and a dangerous storm was coming. She added with a shout, "You older children escort the younger ones!"

Roger Schwartz walked up to his teacher and asked, "What about Jimmy?"

"He should be home by now."

"What if he didn't go home?"

"Where else would he go?"

"His fort?"

"His what?"

"He built hisself a fort in Gruenwald's woods, goes there to be by hisself."

"Him-self, not his-self."

"Yes Miss Olsen."

"It's my job to worry about Jimmy – you go straight home, Mr. Schwartz, and make sure that Billie and Johann get home too." Today is Armistice Day, she thought to herself. All this trouble could have been avoided if the school board had just given us the day off.

Within three minutes, the children were cutting across fields, climbing fences, walking the lane and watching the sky, and Adeline was alone in the school. As she did at the end of each school day, she washed down the blackboards and swept the floor. A gust of wind slammed the door shut behind her and she started, walking to a window and thinking about Jimmy. Dry leaves blew across the school yard like flocks of frightened birds and swollen, blue-black clouds churned off to the west.

Ten minutes later, Adeline opened the door and cried out, "Mercy!" She closed the door, put on her black cloth coat, and reached in her pocket. A carefully folded piece of paper was wedged between her gloves. She unfolded the paper and read: "I put the mouse under your cup during lunch. I won't do it again. Roger S." She shook her head and said, "Oh dear." I must hurry, she thought, perhaps I can find Jimmy and make sure he's alright.

Adeline stood alongside the flagpole, looked up, and lowered the flag, which snapped in the wind like rifle shots. She thought, it's a good twenty degrees colder than when I stood here with Mr. Anderson and getting colder by the minute. A drop of rain slapped against the back of her coat. I must get going, she thought, or I'll be stranded. She rented a room from her cousin, Carl Lauber, a farmer who lived a mile from school. A Milwaukee girl accustomed to paved sidewalks, trimmed bushes, and city parks, Adeline walked to and from her first teaching job along a gravel road lined by brush, barbed wire, and farm dogs. The Gruenwald's black-and-white collie never let her pass without bounding up to her.

Adeline, the bunched flag under her arm, opened the school door and before she could close it behind her, the wind got by her and lifted a dozen sheets of paper from her desk. Folding the flag, she set it on her desk, tied her scarf around her head, and hurried back to the front door, leaving the scattered papers on the floor. She paused on the front porch, startled to see that the rain had turned to sleet. She locked the door, hurried down Schoolhouse Lane, and turned onto County Trunk D. Tucking her head, she thought, thank God I got that wind to my back – it cuts like a knife. A hundred steps further, she heard voices, looked to her right, and saw Mrs. Gruenwald yelling at her chickens and chasing them toward their coop, and Mr. Gruenwald, in his pasture, shouting, waving his arms, herding his brown-and-white guernseys toward the barn.

Adeline quickened her pace and came alongside Gruenwald's woods. She searched the gray-brown tangle of trees, listening to the branches clack and whip in the wind, noticing a logging trail which led into the woods. I must try to find him, she thought, warn him to get home. At that moment, the clouds opened as if cut by a blade and sleet gushed out, coating the road, trees, her coat and shoes with slush and ice. Turning onto the trail, she hurried between the trees, yelling, "Jimmy! Jiiiiimy!"

A hundred steps into the woods, she thought she heard a truck behind her, but when she turned she could no longer see the road and realized that what she had heard was the sound of the wind high in the trees. Wanting to keep warm, Adeline began to run, yelling every dozen steps, her feet splashing slush. Please God, keep him safe, she prayed. All at once the sleet turned to snow – wet flakes the size of pennies.

Adeline stopped. She could see only ten steps ahead of her. Her lungs burned, her body shook, and she realized that she could not think of Jimmy any longer – she had to take care of herself now, get home, or if she couldn't get home, to the Gruenwald's farmhouse. That's when she saw someone in front of her – a man – ten steps away, bent into the wind.

A terrific gust of wind roared through the woods, knocked

her to her knees and took the world with it. She looked up and could see only driving snow – a whiteout. Did I see a ghost? she wondered, frightened, getting to her feet. Adeline yelled "Help!" but she could hardly hear herself and was sure that no one else could hear her. She wanted to run, but where?

A hand grabbed her arm. Looking up, she saw Jimmy's face a foot from her own. He yelled something at her, which she could not hear, then pulled her next to him and began taking small steps forward, Adeline allowing his lead. Jimmy kept the snow and wind to their right and held out his arm ahead of him, touching tree trunks and limbs before he could see them. Suddenly he stopped, yelled, and moved behind his teacher. Adeline reached out her hand, felt something, and thought, some sort of wall! Jimmy put his hands around his teacher's ice-crusted scarf, lowered her head, and guided her through a canvas door. She fell to her hands and knees, and he put his hand on her rump and pushed her in, tripping over her as he entered.

"We made it," he said, breathing hard. Adeline got to her knees, wrapped her arms around herself, and glanced around, blinking, amazed to find herself in a dark room no larger than her bedroom closet, with a roof four feet off a dirt floor, a wall cupboard, one six-inch window, logs for stools, and a steel bucket stove. Adeline's whole body began to shiver and jerk like it wasn't hers any more. Jimmy blew into his hands, grabbed some tinder sticks, and said, "You sit here by my stove, Miss Olsen, and I'll lay us a fire. We ain't going nowhere for a while." She did not notice his wrong usage.

The fire caught, cracking and spitting, but the wind pushed

a lot of smoke back down the stovepipe and into the fort, forcing Adeline and Jimmy to close their eyes. As the fire grew hotter, the draft improved, the smoke cleared, and the fort warmed. Adeline held her hands an inch from the stove, but her lips remained blue, and she did not stop shivering. Jimmy looked at his teacher and said, "You best take off them clothes that's wet, Miss Olsen, or you'll never warm up. You can wear my coat."

"All my clothes are soaked," she said.

"Then they all got to come off." Jimmy helped Adeline take off her iced coat and scarf, then in order to give her privacy, turned away and began arranging the pile of logs and kindling. Adeline unbuttoned her wool sweater, pulled it off, unclasped her bra, removed it, and put on Jimmy's long barn coat, the rough wool liner scratching her bare back, neck, and breasts. She kicked off her shoes, unbuttoned her skirt from top to bottom, and unsnapped her nylons from her garters. After peeling off her stockings, she pulled her knees to her chest and wrapped his coat around her body like a blanket.

Jimmy shoved another log into the stove and both sat without speaking, huddling close to the stove. The wind gusted against the fort and whistled through the cracks in the walls. Chunks of ice fell from swaying tree limbs onto the fort roof. Adeline asked, "Is this as warm as it gets?"

Jimmy looked out the window at the swirling, blowing snow. "I reckon so."

"You're shivering without your coat," Adeline said.

"I ain't bad off. I can take a lot."

"How did you find me?"

"I heard you yell."

"Above this wind?"

"Yes, Miss Olsen. You got a loud voice." Adeline smiled and shook her head like a dog shakes water, and little chunks of ice struck Jimmy and the walls.

By five o'clock, they could no longer see out the window and relied on the orange light flickering out of the stove's door. A fierce gust of wind hit the fort, rattled the stovepipe, and fluttered Adeline's hanging clothes. Jimmy said, "I ain't never seen a storm this bad come on this quick."

Adeline asked, "How long will your wood last?"

"Till dawn if we's lucky."

"Your Mama know about this fort?"

"No, ma'am. You the first girl knows about it."

"You think she's worried about you?"

He shrugged his shoulders. "She got all she can do with my baby sister."

"You worried about them?"

"I'm the man of the house now."

"What about your Pa?"

"He ain't around much since the baby come along." Jimmy turned and reached through the fort's canvas door for a handful of snow, which he mounded into a tin cup and set on the stove. He opened the wall cupboard door and said, "I got a jar of Ma's pickles. A jar of crab apples. And a jar of venison." He pulled out two jars and opened them. With their fingers, they ate slices of thick, soft venison and green, sour pickles.

After their meal, Adeline said, "People are going to die in this blizzard. My cousin, Carl, went duck hunting on the Mississippi – Drakes Bay, somewhere like that. I doubt he even took a decent coat with him." She put her hands over her face.

Jimmy lifted the cup of melted snow off the stove, took a sip, and held it to his teacher. "Good and hot, Miss Olsen," he said. She let her hands drop from her face and wrapped them around the cup.

After a long silence, Adeline said, "I'm sorry I hit you today."

Jimmy shrugged. "I had it coming."

"No. I just didn't know what else to do. Besides, I know now who put that mouse under my cup."

He glanced up at her and back at the fire in the stove. Orange light danced across his face. "I do bad things I don't get caught at, so sometimes I got to get caught doing bad things I didn't do." His logic disturbed her. She thought, he's figured out a way to accept any suffering.

"Your Pa beat you?" she asked quietly.

He nodded, squinting his eyes as if to see something in the flames.

"I won't hit you again, Jimmy, no matter what you do."

He looked at his teacher, surprised by such a promise. He asked, "What if I put a rat in your desk drawer?"

Adeline knew she was being tested. "A live one or a dead one?" she asked.

Jimmy smiled and said, "A live one and a dead one – and the dead one stunk to high heaven!"

Adeline laughed and said, "I'd scream. I'd yell. I'd have you get rid of the rats. I'd have you clean the outhouses and rake the school yard...." Quietly, she added, "But I would not hit you." Suddenly, her body let down and Adeline put her head between her knees and slept while Jimmy tended the fire. The wind blew all night, as if circling the earth and returning again and again and again.

An hour before dawn, Jimmy touched Adeline's shoulder and said, "Miss Olsen, I got to get more wood."

Adeline raised her head from her knees, blinked, and said, "Wait a minute." She took her clothes off the wall and using his big, loose coat as a dressing room, she put on her bra, blouse, and skirt underneath it, then took off his coat. Next, she tied her stockings and sweater end to end and tied one end to Jimmy's ankle. She put the coat around his shoulders, grabbed the clothes-rope, and said, "You got about ten feet – that's all. Get what you can. There ought to be branches on the roof." They crawled to the door on their knees, and Jimmy lifted a smooth stone off the canvas door corner and was gone. Adeline held the sleeve of her damp sweater, which stretched tight in her grip as Jimmy, blinded by wind-driven snow and dark, plunged his hands through the snow on the roof and around his feet. Five minutes later, he crawled back into the fort with an armful of sticks, branches, and a rotted stump which he had kicked free. Even though he was shivering worse than she, he took off his coat, shook off the snow, and gave it back to his teacher.

After first light, Adeline and Jimmy ate the remaining venison slices and half a quart of crab apples. The wind still whistled through the cracks in the fort, but the snow had let up, and by mid-morning, Jimmy could see the lay of the woods through the fort window. About noon, he left the fort without the clothes-rope tied to his ankle. Snow had drifted to the roof on the windward side of the fort, and he kicked through the waist-deep snow and pulled up ice-coated branches with his boot. He cut four or five ash saplings with his pocketknife, glancing often at the gunmetal-blue clouds, wondering if they held more snow. Back in the fort, Adeline asked him, "How is it?"

"Snow's to my waist most places and wind is still bad."

Adeline said, "Maybe we ought to get out of the woods before the snow starts again."

"Snow's too deep to get far," he said, "but I'll take care of that. You keep the fire going." Working fast, Jimmy took out his pocketknife, pulled a small nest of barn twine out of the cupboard, bent each long sapling into an oval, and lashed the ends together. Next, he cut cross-slats and lashed six to each oval sapling. "Miss Olsen," he said, handing her his knife, "you got to cut off my shirt sleeve." Jimmy cut the sleeve into long strips and used them to lash her feet and his to the snowshoes as Adeline put on her scarf and gloves.

Even with snowshoes, they sunk up to their knees. Adeline fell three times and her coat pockets were full of snow before she learned how to widen and slow her steps so that she didn't lay one snowshoe on top of the other. Jimmy in the lead, they snowshoed down the logging trail, knowing they had to find shelter quickly. Jimmy turned to Adeline and yelled, "Gruenwald's ain't far!" She nodded, put her head down, and put one snowshoe in front of the other until Jimmy stopped and she stepped onto his snowshoe and bumped against his back. Adeline looked over his shoulder and saw what had stopped him, a scene she'd remember the rest of her life: Diedrich Gruenwald, sitting with his back against a maple trunk, still, his legs covered with snow, eyes open and hard as stone, looking across his woods. A cry came out of Adeline's mouth and was carried away by the wind.

Jimmy stood motionless, his mouth open, no longer a man leading a woman out of danger but an eighth-grade boy brought to a standstill by true calamity. Mr. Gruenwald had been one of the few men in Jimmy's life who had treated him kindly, had once said to him, "I seen you built a fort in my woods – I guess we's true neighbors now, you and me. You come over anytime you need something."

Adeline grabbed Jimmy's head with both gloved hands and turned it toward her until his brown eyes looked into her blue eyes with nothing but the wind between their faces. "There's nothing we can do for him!" she yelled, knowing it was time for her to take the lead.

They walked out of the trees and onto the drifted, empty road, a wind chute. Adeline pulled her scarf across her cheeks and mouth and squinted, looking for the white farm-house. The blowing snow obscured the house, but she could see the top of the spruce and red barn next to the house, an eighth of a mile away. Two hundred steps, she thought. About halfway to the farmhouse, Jimmy grabbed Adeline's arm and pointed to the windswept pasture to their left. Four of Gruenwald's guernseys stood against a wooden fence gate, rumps to the wind, heads under drifting snow as if rooting for grass, frozen stiff.

Adeline and Jimmy walked into the vacant barnyard. No collie. Two cows which had found their way to the barn stood inside the open barn door, looking out, lowing, desperate to be milked and fed. Adeline thought, thank God something's alive! The house looked empty, but when they snowshoed into the yard, Mrs. Gruenwald, who had been watching the road, threw open the door and ran toward them, shouting, stumbling, rising, stumbling. Adeline and Jimmy each took her by an arm and walked her back to the house, her body nearly limp. Once the three were in the entryway, Adeline seated Florence on the steps. As soon as Florence caught her breath she cried out, "Diedrich went out to bring in the cows and never come home!"

Adeline glanced at Jimmy, sat next to Florence on the step, took her hand, and said, "We found him. In the woods." Florence's eyes flashed open and one sob blew out of her mouth like a gust of wind. Closing her eyes and mouth, she plunged her head into Adeline's bosom, and Adeline began to rock back and forth, their two bodies, one. Watching the women, Jimmy backed through the door, turned, and walked to the barn. The cows saw Jimmy coming toward them, turned, and hurried to their milking stalls like excited children.

After milking and feeding the cows, Jimmy set the pails of milk in the barn door and returned to the farmhouse where he found Adeline in the kitchen, preparing a pot of coffee. "Miss Olsen, I know you got to take care of Mrs. Gruenwald, but I got to get home and check on Ma and the baby." Adeline did not know what to do. She could not leave Florence, but neither could she allow Jimmy to return home alone – God knows what he'll find there, she thought. Jimmy turned to leave and Adeline saw Norman Bruderman, the farmer to the north, ski up to the Gruenwald's door. Five minutes after his arrival, Jimmy and Adeline left Florence in his care, bundled into Diedrich's coats, scarves, and caps, and snowshoed the empty road toward Jimmy's home, into the wind.

As they crossed Schoolhouse Lane, Adeline stopped and

looked toward the school. The lane was hidden, now part of the drifted fields. The schoolyard oaks were bare and the snow was drifted to the bottom of the tall windows against the school's west wall. Adeline shook her head and thought, might as well be January. She looked again at Jimmy, who had not stopped, put her face down, and tried to catch him. He angled off the road and cut across a large field toward a wooded ravine – Adeline fifty steps behind him. Where is he going? she wondered. She yelled to him, but he could not hear her, and he soon disappeared among the trees, which left her following his tracks.

A hundred steps into the woods, Jimmy's tracks turned onto what looked to her like a narrow lane through the trees. She looked down the lane and saw Jimmy standing at the edge of a small clearing, looking back at her, waiting for her, and ahead of him, a cabin of rough logs, drifted to the eaves. Breathing hard, she snowshoed to his side and they studied the cabin. No movement. No tracks. No smoke. Adeline asked, "Is that your home?" Jimmy nodded, thinking again of Gruenwald and the frozen cattle. She added, "Let's hope for the best."

Jimmy put his shoulder to the cabin door, pushed it open and clomped his snowshoes onto the board floor. Adeline entered behind him and they looked around the frigid, one-room cabin: an iron bed in one corner, stripped of blankets; a black, empty stove with the door swung open; three cots in one corner; a tall, eight-drawer bureau with one drawer pulled out and lined with leaves, the baby's crib; and in another corner, a chair, piled high with quilts and blankets which suddenly moved and rose, draping a figure who came straight for Jimmy and knocked him to his butt. A woman's voice, mean and loud: "I give you up for dead!"

Dazed, Jimmy sat on the floor between Adeline and the draped woman. A baby started to cry from underneath the quilt.

"Is she okay?" Jimmy asked.

"No thanks to you. Get us some wood and get a fire going. We's half froze."

Adeline said, "He saved my life."

"Who the hell are you?"

"His schoolteacher."

"His school days are done. He's got us to take care of now." Adeline could see that there was no room in this woman for tenderness, and that she herself was a lot like this woman, and her school a lot like this bare, little cabin. She thought, I must make room in me, in my school, for tenderness – I must learn how to teach it along with fractions and script and spelling. But how? She looked at Jimmy and thought, he's my teacher now.

Four days later, Adeline stood in front of her students for the first time since the blizzard. The school yard was full of puddles, mud, and patches of soggy snow. A pile of black coal lay next to the white building, a shovel standing in the pile. Jimmy's desk was empty and she wondered if he was just absent for the day or done with school, as his mother had ordered. She decided that she'd visit their cabin again after school. "Welcome back, students," Adeline said quietly. "Thank the Lord you're all safe and sound."

After school, Adeline stood beneath the flagpole and lowered the limp flag. She heard shoveling and saw Jimmy standing alongside the pile of coal, barechested, shoveling chunks of coal into the woodshed. She smiled and waved at him, and he nodded. Behind him, Mr. Anderson's black Buick bounced down the rutted lane, splashing water and mud. She knew that he had news for her about her cousin, Carl, who was still missing, and she could tell that the news was not good by the fierce way he held his mouth and gripped the steering wheel. She looked up at the blue sky and imagined her cousin sitting in his skiff, gun across his lap, head back, face to the sky, waiting for a flock of mallards to set their wings and come in close.

STRAWBERRY MONEY

For seventy years, Iris had denied herself small pleasures, especially if they cost money, but when she saw the glider on Luloff's showroom floor something in her shifted, and she said to herself, "For heaven's sakes, the world won't come to an end if I spend a little money on myself!"

Iris found her husband in Hardware, holding what she thought was a handgun, but when he looked up, he said, "An electric screwdriver. If that don't beat all." She led Harold to the glider and he ran his hands over the varnished maple frame. "Good and solid," he said. "But looks to be a hard seat."

"I'd make a cushion, of course," she said.

He flipped over the cardboard price tag and said gravely, "Two hundred forty-nine dollars." The tone of his voice reminded her of her mother, who had told her time and again, "A woman who spends money on herself might as well ask the devil to dance."

"Won't cost you a cent," Iris said. "I got my strawberry money." They left Luloff's without buying the glider or the electric screwdriver.

The old couple got in their dark blue Skylark and drove slowly down Main Street, past Clara's Market, a corner grocery with aisles so narrow that two people had to turn sideways to pass. Clara stood under the front awning, arms folded across her aproned chest, watching each car go by. Harold lifted his right-hand index finger from the steering wheel, his way of waving. "Harold – pull over," Iris said. "We can't just drive by Clara without buying something."

Clara took Iris by the hand and the two women walked into the market. Iris returned to the car with a ten-pound bag of flour in the crook of her arm, which she set onto the seat between her and Harold. A tiny cloud of white flour poofed from the bag and settled on the blue vinyl like dust.

At the edge of town, where houses gave way to cornfields, the freshly laid asphalt steamed from a recent cloudburst and the Skylark's tires whooshed and hummed down the wet road. Three cars passed them and Harold raised his index finger to each driver. Without signaling his intentions, he slowed and turned onto County E. Once, Iris had asked him why he never used his turn signals. He had looked at her in amazement, saying "Why should I? Every fool around here knows where I'm headed."

Iris plugged in the percolator and walked through their front room, out the screen door, and onto their front porch, which Harold had added to the house after their daughter left for Chicago but which they had never furnished. Ivy, like green walls, enfolded the house but was carefully trimmed back at the windows and doors like brush at the edge of a pasture. Iris smelled the approaching rain and watched a pair of robins fuss and flutter at the bird bath. She leaned against a porch post and thought, how nice it will be to sit on that glider with Harold, rock a little, watch day pass into night. Her mother's voice spoke again, "We sat on empty milk cans on our porch. That was good enough for us."

Four years earlier, Iris and Harold had given up the hard work of the farm and rented their pasture and cropland to neighbors, but Iris had never given up the hard work of picking strawberries each June at the Sturdevents' farm, just a mile south on County E. Nobody picked strawberries like Iris. Her hands moved among the tender plants like snakes, searching, grasping, snipping, red as the berries she picked by day's end, waving off mosquitoes, cramps, and weariness. She picked eight or ten hours a day, resting only on rain days and the Lord's Day. The other pickers, teenagers from the surrounding farms, could not keep up with her, their hard young bodies in shorts and tennis shoes outdistanced by "Old Lady Gau" in the cotton dress, apron, and sunbonnet. With a good row, she could fill four boxes an hour. For each box, Mr. Sturdevent handed her a crisp dollar bill, which she folded and pushed to the bottom of her apron pocket.

Iris kept her strawberry money in a powder-blue sugar bowl, a wedding gift from her mother. She stored the bowl in her second dresser drawer, tucked under her slips like an egg in a nest, hidden even from her husband, who looked for it at least once a year but had never found it. One year, he had opened that very dresser drawer but could not bring himself to plunge his dirty hands into his wife's white underwear.

Iris spent her strawberry money only on other people. One year, she had sent three hundred dollars to Jim Snyder, Channel Five news anchor, with a note: "Please send this money to Mexico to help all those poor people suffering from the earthquake." He had sent her a note of thanks on Channel Five stationary, which she kept under the sugar bowl. Another year, Iris had sent the money to Moravian missionaries in Brazil who had needed a pickup truck for their work. As thanks, they had sent her a photo of their new, red Datsun. Under the sugar bowl. Last year, she had bought two Schwinns for her Chicago grandsons, and her daughter had sent her a photo of the boys on their bikes, waving. Under the sugar bowl. This year, she thought, I'll buy that glider for myself. I'll get all dressed up and have Harold take a picture of me sitting on it, and I'll put that picture under the sugar bowl.

On the first morning of strawberry season, Iris got behind the wheel of the Skylark and drove south, toward the Sturdevents'. She was driving past her cousin Ethel's farm when the sun broke through the clouds, reminding her that she might need her bonnet. Perhaps I put it on the back seat, she thought, as she looked over her shoulder. "Clank! Thud!" Iris wrenched her head forward, clobbered the brake, and skidded to a stop on the roadside grass. Taking a deep breath, Iris put the car in Park, turned off the ignition, opened the door, and walked to the front of the car. "Oh dear!" she said. Her right headlight was smashed; the hood, scratched. She dropped to her berry-picking position and looked under the car. "Oh my God!" she said, not given to using the Lord's name in such a manner.

Ethel came up behind Iris and asked, "Iris, are you okay?"

Startled, Iris looked behind her and sighed, "Oh!" Ethel helped her to her feet and Iris said, "I'm sorry. I'm so sorry."

"It's only a mailbox, Iris. Don't worry."

Arm in arm, the women walked to the house. Ethel helped Iris into Ben's La-Z-Boy and brought her a glass of ice water. Iris took the glass with both hands, turned to her cousin and said as much as asked, "You won't tell Harold, now, will you?"

After her hands stopped trembling, Iris drove to town, slowly, her eyes on the road and her hands at ten o'clock and two o'clock on the steering wheel. She turned down the only alley in Kiel and parked alongside a cement block garage. A tall, thin man in paint-sprayed coveralls came out to greet her. Without telling him what had happened, Iris told him what needed to be repaired. She stood by his side for two hours as he installed a new headlight and touched up the hood. "I'll pay you in cash, Mr. Donovan," she said. "If you can wait until the end of strawberry season."

That evening, Iris phoned her daughter, Donna, in Chicago and told her about the accident. Donna scolded Iris, "Mom, you shouldn't pay for those repairs out of your strawberry money. Call the insurance company first thing in the morning."

"Oh, I don't want to bother them with my mistake."

"Mom, you pay insurance premiums for the right to bother them." Both she and her daughter knew that the insurance company, along with Harold, would never learn about her mistake.

After strawberry season, Iris drove to town, alone, her sugar bowl beside her on the seat like a passenger. She handed Mr. Donovan a stack of two hundred and ten one-dollar bills, which left her thirty-one. On the way out of town, she stopped at Luloff's, pulled an orange tape-measure from her purse, and measured the glider seat.

That evening, Iris knelt in front of a green battered trunk which she used to store her fabric scraps. Eighty years earlier, the trunk had held all of her mother's worldly goods on the steamship passage from Hamburg to New York. Iris lifted the strapped cover and looked through the fabric scraps, settling on a piece of maroon corduroy which she had bought years earlier, on sale as a remnant. After watching Jim Snyder deliver the ten o'clock news, Harold turned off the television and the lights and looked in on Iris.

"You coming to bed then?" he asked.

"You go on. I want to get this done."

"What is it?"

"You'll see in the morning." She worked past midnight, the first time she could remember being up that late since New Year's Eve.

At breakfast, she set the completed cushion on the kitchen table, a centerpiece between their bowls of oatmeal. Harold raised his eyebrows and repeated his earlier warning, "Two hundred forty-nine dollars." Iris thought, Lord, give me twelve days of raspberry picking and I'll buy that glider so help me.

Iris did not usually pick raspberries, the season being hot and short, but she picked fourteen days without a complaint until the berries were so few and far between that she told Mr. Sturdevent, "Let the birds have the rest. They have to eat too." She drove home that day with one hand on the steering wheel and the other buried in her apron pocket, counting the dollar bills. Whenever she passed a mailbox, she steered to the center of the road.

While Iris stewed some tomatoes and rice for lunch, Harold plowed under the first crop of garden beans with his walking tractor. Three summers earlier, the tractor muffler had broken off and Harold had never replaced it, pricing but never purchasing a new one, so the little Briggs & Stratton engine roared and stank. At noon, Harold came into the kitchen, frowned, and pointed at his head. Iris said, "You got another headache from that tractor, didn't you? Why don't you just buy a new muffler?"

"I won't pay no eleven dollars for a little bitty muffler," Harold said.

"Harold Peter Gau, you're the cheapest man in the county, maybe the world."

"I'm going to lie down for a bit. Bring me some aspirin."

"Aspirin costs money too!"

The Culligan repair truck pulled up the gravel driveway and parked in front of the empty porch. Iris opened the screen door and studied the young man who got out of the truck and walked toward her. "I'm Mrs. Gau," she said.

"I'm Carl Schneider, your new Culligan man." He figured that she wanted to know about her old Culligan man, so he added, "Fred finally retired."

She nodded and said, "Good for him." Not able to place Carl's face or name, she asked, "You're not from town, then?"

"From Sheboygan. But you might know my great uncle, Hans Schneider.

"Oh! And how is Hans?"

Iris escorted Carl into the basement. He worked on the water softener in silence for several minutes and shook his head just before he looked at her, so she knew he had bad news. "Iris, you need a new motor. She's burned up."

"How can that be?" she asked, startled. "It's nearly new." Two years earlier, changing water tables had forced Harold and Iris to deepen their well by one hundred and ten feet, and their well-digger had insisted that they add a water softener, or, he had said, "Your water will taste like rocks." Harold still complained about the unexpected expense: "Fifteen hundred for that well, another three hundred for that softener. Robbery."

Carl asked, "Mrs. Gau, how often do you add salt to the bin?"

"I pour in a pitcher of salt every Monday morning," she said.

He smiled at her like a man smiles at a woman who doesn't know better. "You could pour a pitcher in here every day and it wouldn't be enough. You need to pour a hundred pounds in here and keep it full."

"What will a new one cost?" she asked, weakly.

Taking a pencil, Carl scribbled some figures on the salt-bin lid. "Two sixty-four, installed."

"Two *hundred* sixty-four?"

"I got one in the truck."

Accepting the blow, she lowered her head and said, "I'll pay you in cash. And don't go waking my husband. He does not need to lose sleep over this." Iris climbed the stairs, walked quietly into her bedroom – past her sleeping husband – and opened her second dresser drawer. She shoved aside her slips and picked up the sugar bowl with both hands, holding it in front of her like a chalice.

Later that week, Iris drove past the berry patch on her way

to the Town Line Moravian Church, the glider cushion beside her on the front seat. Occasional drops of rain splattered against her windshield like fat, soft bugs. She pulled into the gravel parking lot and parked alongside a dozen other cars, each facing the storm to the north, each belonging to a woman in her quilting circle. A clipped, lush lawn surrounded the white frame church like a green moat holding back the advance of cornfields and woods. On one side of the church, tombstones rose out of the lawn like rows of gray, manicured shrubs. To the north, thunderheads billowed, darkened, and rumbled.

Iris planned to join her friends in the church basement, but first she put the cushion under her arm and walked into the sanctuary, a simple, square room with white walls, clear, tall windows and blonde oak pews, enough for a hundred. On the altar: a dozen wilted, dark purple gladiolas in a green glass vase. Iris looked around the sanctuary before she placed her cushion for two on the pew where she and Harold sat on Sunday mornings, hip to hip, as far from the pulpit as they could get. Iris believed that one had to break in a new cushion like one had to break in a new book binding, so she sat on it lightly, afraid of crushing it. How soft this is! she thought. I feel like I'm floating! This will take some getting used to!

Iris folded her hands in her lap and listened to the storm. Rain began to pound the tin roof so hard that it sounded to her like Harold had started his walking tractor on the roof. Lightning flashed, followed by cracks of thunder so fierce that Iris winced. Below her, the women chatted and laughed. Iris thought, I've got twelve dollars left in my sugar bowl. I'll buy

Harold his muffler. Turning to her left, she looked out a window and leaned forward – careful not to crush the cushion – until she could see the granite gravestone of her mother, visible only as a blur through the sheet-rain. Breaking her silence, she said, "I guess you didn't want me to have that glider," in a way which left her wondering whether she had spoken to herself, her mother in the graveyard, or God in heaven.

THEIR PA TOLD ME, "As boys they was thick as jam – looked pretty near like twins with their mama's blue eyes and blond hair and skin so fair they got sunburn in the rain." Their Ma said, "When Ivan and Werner was done with school they went to old man Gordon, told him, "We want to save some money and buy your place, farm it as brothers." That was their plan, but like most plans, it didn't hold up to life. Werner fell head over heels for Vivian and asked her to marry him, and before Ivan knew what hit him, Werner bought the Gordon place by himself and was getting it ready for him and his bride. This set Ivan back pretty good, though he never let on. He was like a walking dead man the day of their wedding – refused to give the toast at the reception, just shook his head and looked at his shoes. That hurt Werner good.

Six months later, Ivan and I got married. Vivian came to our wedding alone, without Werner, and Ivan kept his eye out for him, half-hoping he'd show. We bought the Sven-moore place, which butts up against Werner and Vivian's down by the swamp. It's not as nice a place as theirs, but Ivan said, "I'll have it looking better than his in five years."

Not long after our wedding, Ivan and Werner met up at the Lechler's auction and both started bidding on a hay wagon. Ivan had lost the Gordon place to Werner – he was not about to lose that hay wagon to him. Each nodded the price higher until everyone else stopped bidding and watched those two brothers go at it. At nine hundred, Werner turned his back and walked off, most likely laughing. Old Man Lechler got more for that wagon than he got for his tractor! After that, the brothers went out of their way to avoid each other.

The following spring, Werner painted his feed barn the color of a robin's egg. We can see his barn out our kitchen window, so I called Vivian and asked what in earth had gotten into Werner. "You know him," she says, "Always got to have a deal." Well he got a deal alright on forty gallons of paint which he thought was Grey Blue. At home, he opened a bucket, went to get his glasses, and read the label again: Sky Blue! Benson wouldn't give him his money back so he painted the tractor doors, just to see how it looked. Neighbors dropped by to see his sky-blue barn doors. They teased him good, which he didn't take kindly to. He can dish it out but can't take it when it comes back at him. Ivan came by one day, said, "Paint a few clouds on it too." That did it for Werner. He told Ivan to get off our land and painted the whole barn sky blue out of spite. Them two thick-as-jam brothers haven't said one word to the other since that minute.

Just cause Werner and Ivan stopped talking didn't mean we women stopped talking. Vivian and me talked till *we* was sky blue, even worked out a way to get them back together through their cousin, Hugo, but when Ivan got wind of this, he said, "Keep your nose in your own goddam business, woman!" He don't use that language with me much. Their ma and pa talked too. Their pa threw up his hands and said, "They act like they ain't flesh and blood!" Ralph Anderson, our neighbor to the north, told Ivan that he could understand why a fella might stop talking to a brother who would go off and paint his barn sky blue, so I knew the neighbors was talking too.

Come October, a big buck moved into our cedar swamp, and Ivan perked right up. "A ten-pointer," he said. "I seen him by our apple tree. Biggest buck around here in years." Ivan started dumping all our bad apples near his deer stand.

I told him, "In case you forgot, last year the warden fined Warren Miller for doing just what you're doing – deer baiting." He threw up his hands and said, "Got to dump bad apples somewhere, don't I?" When that man has his mind made up might as well talk to the wind. He was going to get that buck, no two ways about it.

On opening day of deer season, we got up extra early. I started a pot of coffee and opened the back door. The cold went right through me. A light snow covered the lawn around the house like a blanket. Ivan did his chores, pulled his red coverall over his bibs, and said, "Venison steaks tonight! Get out the onions and potatoes!" I opened the back door and watched him walk toward the swamp with his rifle over his shoulder, his boots squeaking against the snow.

At first light, I heard a shot in the swamp. Ten minutes later, a second. An hour later, Ivan came home, sat in his kitchen chair, hung his head. I said, "You look like you just lost your crop."

"I did," he said. "I shot once. His four legs went out from under him and he dropped, dead before he hit the ground I figure. I walk up to that ten-pointer, put down my rifle, and get out my knife. I kneel beside him and I'll be goddammed – he picks his head off the ground and looks me in the eye. Two bounds and he's in the cedars. I give him a few minutes before I take his trail, figure he'll lie down when he feels safe and never get up. There's a lot of blood on the snow, big, dark spots – liver shot, I reckon, as I follow his blood trail into the swamp. That's when I hear a shot ahead of me." Ivan frowned and pointed out the window toward his brother's place as if he was pointing to hell. "That buck jumps his fence but I don't let that stop me – I keep on his trail, until I hear that old pickup of his drive off down the logging trail. By the time I get to my buck he's nothin' but a pile of hot guts in the snow." Ivan looked up at me and added, "I was so mad I kicked them guts all over his woods."

The Lord put a thought in my mind. I started banging cupboard doors like I was good and mad, which got Ivan's attention. "What's got into you now?"

"I'll tell you what's got into me, Mr. Ivan Johnson! That no good brother of yours got your buck hanging in his sky blue barn!"

"Jesus, woman!" he yelled, "I thought you liked my brother. I thought you'd probably ring him up and say, 'Great shot, Werner!'" That was the first time in two years I heard him use his brother's name.

"What are you going to do about it?" I demanded.

He got quiet and looked out the window. I shut up. Next thing I knew he jumped from his seat like that downed buck, ran out the door, got in his truck, spun his tires on the snow and gravel, was gone.

I waited. Ten minutes later the phone rang. Werner says, "Better come over here right away." I went. Ivan was laid out on their front room couch, eyes closed, hands across his red jacket.

"He's out cold."

I got upset and said, "You better do some explaining."

"He come barging over here and says, 'I drew first blood! That buck's mine!' I says, 'No way. I killed him. I gut him. I hung him. He's mine.' He shoves me like he used to when we was kids and I decked him.... That's all." Werner put his big-knuckled hands in his pockets and looked at the floor. His blond bangs fell across his face, hiding his eyes. I think, he's about as handsome as they come, him and his brother both. Now you'd think I'd get worse upset, but I got calm as a summer night.

"Why'd you call me?" I asked.

"A woman's got to nurse him."

"Where's Vivian?"

"Off shopping in town – where she always is when I need her."

"You hit him. You nurse him." I turned on my heels, walked into the kitchen and poured me a hot cup of coffee.

A minute later, Werner came into the kitchen. He filled a wash basin with cold water and got a small towel out of the cupboard. He went back in the front room, and I watched him from the doorway, holding my mug with both hands. He sat on the couch next to Ivan, dipped the towel in the water, folded it into a square, and laid it across Ivan's right cheek. It felt so good to see those brothers together again that I could hardly take it. I put on my coat and went out for some air.

It was cold, damp to the bone. I looked up. A quilt of gray clouds lay across the sky. More snow tonight, I thought. A flock of Canadian geese flew over Werner's barn, low, heading south, their lonesome honking bouncing between the frozen ground and those dark clouds. I thought, I bet those geese are looking for blue sky and got fooled by that barn! The tractor doors was open and that buck hung by his antlers for all the world to see, so I walked over to him. A drop of dark blood fell from his white tail onto the barn floor, and I laid my cheek against his rough, manly hair.

ICE NEIGHBORS

Lake Winnebago was as huge and empty as a winter prairie, except for shanties clustered across the ice like tiny villages. Six shanties had been stolen from the ice, "Just up and disappeared in the black of night," as told by one ice neighbor to another. A mile out from the Brothertown landing, five men in bulky parkas stood in a small circle on the ice, facing one another.

"I say we call Sheriff Henke, see what he can do."

"Henke says there's a tausend shanties out here, says he can't do much."

"Must be kids. No growed man would steal another man's house."

"Don't fool yourselves. There's money in shanties. I sold my old shanty for three hundred to a guy from Oshkosh."

Oscar, the group's elder at seventy, pulled off his wool cap and spit onto the ice at the center of the circle. Loose snow blew across the ice in waves and stung his bare scalp and hands. "Let's give that thief a little surprise if he comes calling in our neck of the woods."

After working out Oscar's plan, the men turned away from

one another and slid their carpet-thick boots across the ice toward their own shanties. From the outside, Oscar's shanty
looked like a large outhouse with two tiny windows, but from
the inside, "she," as Oscar referred to it, looked like a home:
painted walls, canvas curtains, a tiny corner table of yellow
formica, a bookshelf stacked with Outdoor Life magazines,
and two upended nail kegs, one for Oscar, one for a neighbor. His five-pronged spear, tied to a thirty-foot retrieve line,
leaned against a shanty wall. Half the floor of his ice home
was plywood, the other half a window-sized hole cut through
two feet of ice. Dark water filled the hole to the brim like coffee in a white cup.

Near sunset, Oscar stepped out of his shanty onto the ice,
locked the shanty door and tugged the lock, twice. Above the
door, a handpainted sign read: "Pass Me Not O Gentle Sturgeon." Last season, a seventy-seven inch, one-hundred fifteen
pound sturgeon did not pass him by and ended up next to
Oscar on the front page of the Tri-County Record, hanging
by its prehistoric tail. In the photo, Oscar wore a black fur
coat which hung to his ankles. Oscar drove his pickup off the
ice and headed home. That night, his house rafters shifted
and cracked from the cold.

The next morning, Oscar followed his wife around the
house as she watered her ferns and told her about his plan to
surprise the shanty thief. He added, "Tonight's my night,
Ethel."

"Go on!" she said, alarmed. "It'll be ten below tonight. I
don't like you out there all night by your lonesome."

"We each took a night, Ethel. Besides," he added with a
smile, "my blood's thicker than my truck antifreeze and you

know it." Oscar laid out his clothes and supplies on the bed, including his pa's old coat, a black bear hide sewn fur-side out into a long coat which weighed twenty-five pounds, the coat Oscar had been wearing when he plunged his spear through the water and into the oily white flesh of that seventy-seven incher.

Ten above zero. Noon. Oscar eased his pickup down the steep ramp at the Brothertown landing and rolled onto the ice. His shanty stood one mile from Winnebago's east shore, ten miles from any other shore. He parked in front of a shanty which had a ribbon of white smoke rising from a tiny tin chimney. Oscar rolled down his window and tapped his horn. A man with long blond hair stuck his head out the shanty door. John was a generation younger than his ice neighbors, the only one in their ice village who wore sunglasses and heated his shanty with a woodstove – which got him teased: "Ya, pretty soon he'll have a gas furnace in there." "When we was your age, we was out here in short sleeves." John's large, pouty lips cracked and bled while he was on the ice so Oscar had nicknamed him Lips, and the name stuck. Oscar shouted, "You got that thief tied up in there?" Lips smiled and motioned Oscar to join him in his shanty. After visiting in front of Lips' stove, Oscar stood, said, "Hell. It's too warm for me in here," and drove to his shanty. He unloaded his clothes and equipment and drove his pickup a quarter of a mile from his shanty, parking it behind a waist-high snowdrift which had built up along an ice crack. No one will see it here, he thought.

Back in his shanty, Oscar pulled the canvas curtains across the windows. His eyes adjusted to the dark, and he could see his red-and-white wooden decoy – carved into the shape of a fish – dangling just inches from the sandy bottom, eight feet below his spear hole. Oscar sat on a nail keg and watched the underwater scene, alert for movement. The water glowed with pale green light, as if sunlight had been trapped under the ice at freezeup. From time to time that afternoon, a sauger or perch swam up to Oscar's decoy, nosed it, and swam away, but no giant sturgeon glided into his view. The February wind gusted against his ice house, a lonely, happy sound to Oscar.

At four o'clock, Lips knocked on Oscar's door. Without rising from his nail keg, Oscar yelled, "It ain't locked!"

Lips opened the door, stepped inside, closed the door behind him, and sat on the second nail keg. Neither man spoke until their eyes were used to the dark and they could see clearly to the lake bottom.

Without looking up, Oscar asked, "Do any good?"

Lips said, "Ain't seen a fish since Thursday."

"That shanty thief must have stole the fish too."

After ten minutes of watching the water and talking, Lips said, "I got to go home. It's your shift now."

Near dusk, Oscar opened his shanty door and stepped onto the ice. The sun looked like a red ball about to bounce against the line of bare trees on the western shore. He unzipped the fly of his cargo pants and used two hands to find and align the flies of his long underwear. Yellow pee splashed onto the ice, puddled, steamed, and froze. His shadow, twenty-feet tall, stretched toward shore, as if it wanted off the ice before dark. The pickups which had been parked alongside the other shanties were gone, the ice village abandoned for the night.

Back in his shanty, Oscar opened the window curtains and lit both stove burners, frying thick slices of Spam and diced potatoes in one skillet, two eggs in the other. It was almost dark as he mopped up the egg yolks with a piece of Wonder Bread, so he lit a thick white candle and set it on the formica counter. This gave him enough light to glance at magazine photos but kept it dark enough so that he could see across the ice when he looked out.

At nine o'clock, Oscar wiggled into his sheepskin para-trooper pants. He lifted his black coat off a nail on the wall and pulled into that bear hide like it was a new layer of skin. Oscar stepped out of his shanty and into a night so still and clear that he felt like he had stepped into a black-and-white photograph. No wind. No sound. Bitter air burned his face, throat, and lungs. He thought, if God hit this night with a hammer the whole thing would splinter into a million, tiny pieces.

House lights, like strands of Christmas tree lights, sparkled along the eastern shore, the other shores as black as the fur around his body. Oscar checked his neighbor's shanties with the beam of his flashlight, one by one. Looking up, he pointed his flashlight at the North Star, then to the neighboring stars, outlining the Big Dipper with his little beam of light.

Back from his night patrol, Oscar dropped a boat cushion on the plywood floor of his ice home and sat on it, bracing his back against one wall, his feet against the other. The candle flame held back the dark. Glancing at the spear hole next to him, he thought, God save me from rolling into it tonight! The ice cracked and shifted beneath him, searching, like

Oscar, for a comfortable way to spend the night.

Darkness. Oscar woke, stiff and cold. He wiggled his toes, and clapped his mittened hands together several times, but all at once he held still, listening. The voices of two men traveled through the cold like electricity through water. Oscar stood, grabbed his spear, left his dark shanty, and shuffled across the ice toward Lips' shanty. The closer he got to the voices, the lower he bent, finally dropping to all fours, stalking: fifty feet, forty, thirty, spear range. Here, he froze like a predator before the final lunge. His heart beat in his throat and his tail twitched madly. Two men, now in his sight, tilted Lips' shanty against the tailgate of a pickup, lifted the shanty bottom, and slid the upended ice-home onto the empty truck bed. When the tin chimney touched the back of the truck cab, they took off their gloves and lowered their heads. Matches flamed. Cigarettes glowed.

Oscar thought, now or never! He raised himself to his hind legs, held his spear above his head, let out a great roar from the place in his throat where his heart beat, "Rrrrrrrrrrrr-aaaaaaaaa!" and rushed the thieves, who jerked to attention like startled deer and scrambled for the cab of their pickup. The truck's engine belched, and the snow tires spun and whined against the smooth ice. Oscar slid to a stop less than ten feet from the back of the pickup. He reared back and hurled his spear as the neanderthals once must have hurled their spears at those garage-sized mammoths. The spear struck the plywood floor of Lips' shanty with the sound of an axe hitting a frozen stump: *Klunk!*

Lips opened his eyes and sat up in bed at that exact moment, as if Oscar's spear had struck his bed post. He said to his wife, "Something is wrong on the ice. I gotta go." He pulled his parka over his flannel pajamas and stuck his bare feet into his boots.

The thief behind the steering wheel did not realize that his stolen cargo had been impaled but he did realize that he was going nowhere fast, so he let off the gas and his tires slowed and grabbed. The retrieve line in Oscar's hand began to unravel as the truck pulled away from him. Not about to let this one get away, Oscar wrapped the line around his hands like a plow rein and braced himself, ready to jerk the spear and pull the shanty off the truck. The retrieve line tightened and Oscar himself got jerked – almost off his feet, but he kept his balance and slid across the ice on his boot bottoms. The truck picked up speed, twenty, thirty, forty miles an hour across the ice and through the night with Oscar in tow like a water skier behind a speedboat. Bitter wind brought tears to Oscar's eyes but he felt good, strong, roaring again, "Rrrrrrrraaaaaaaaa!" Moments later, his boots caught on a bit of caked snow and Oscar became airborne, parallel to the ice like a flag flapping in the wind. He hit the ice belly-first and let out a "Whuff!" But he did not let go.

The truck hit the Brothertown ramp at thirty and Lips' shanty bounced into the air. Oscar, still on his belly, released the line as the shanty crashed to the ramp behind the truck, and he slid to a stop halfway up the ramp, just behind the shanty. Winded but unhurt, he got on his feet and watched the pickup – its lights still off – turn onto the shoreline highway. The snow tires began to hum as it picked up speed. Oscar sat on the overturned shanty, blowing like a winded animal. After a few minutes, he dusted the snow off his belly fur, knelt beside his spear, and worked it out of the shanty floor. Spear in hand, he stood, looked at the sweep of stars and thought, how can the night can be so bright and dark at the same time?

As Oscar walked toward the public-landing pay phone to call Lips, he heard again the hum of snow tires on the shore-line highway. He saw headlights slow and turn onto Ramp Road. Certain that the thieves were returning for their booty, Oscar hurried back to the shanty and crouched behind it, ready to defend it once more. Lips stopped his Bronco just before the ramp, puzzled. He got out and walked down the ramp in the beam of his headlights to see what was blocking his way. Recognizing his shanty, he crossed himself, reached down, and touched the bent tin chimney as if he were touching the forehead of a wounded friend. Oscar growled, stood, raised his spear, and roared again, "Rrrrrraaaaaa!"

MUSKIES AND VIRGINS

THE GIRLS SHOWED, which surprised us. Heidi was the most womanly girl who had ever walked toward me on purpose. Blonde and barefoot, she wore cut-offs and a blue blouse, its tails tied in a knot above her summer brown belly. My heart beat in my throat. I straightened up, raised my chin and told myself, you're six-two with sideburns past your ear lobes! You look eighteen! Tina looked a year or two younger than Heidi, sixteen maybe, tall, light-brown hair, blue eyes, a wash of freckles across her nose and cheeks. I caught Dan's eye and he raised his bushy right eyebrow so high that it disappeared behind his bangs.

The four of us sat on the pier and splashed our feet in the stained August water. We had met the girls that morning at Bud and Jill's Grocery, by the magazine rack. When we had asked where they were staying, Heidi had rolled her eyes and said, "With my parents," and added, "At Cozy Shores Resort." I had invited them to visit our musky camp, Zim's Virgin Timber Lodge, which I had come to think of as Zim's Timber Lodge For Virgins, like us.

Heidi crossed her legs and asked, "So where you guys

from?"

Dan pointed south. "Coon Valley, a little town near the Mississippi."

Heidi said, "Tina and I are neighbors, Chicago style. We live in Lake Towers. She's on eight. I'm on thirty." I thought, they probably got more people living in their high-rise than we got in our town.

A black-and-yellow ski boat rounded Piney Point at thirty miles an hour, on plane. Dan declared, "That black beauty is a ninety-horse Mercury, one of the best." When the boat sped past our pier, the girls waved with their hands and feet at the guy in charge of those ninety horses. He looked about twenty, with dark sunglasses, long sandy hair, in charge of the fastest boat on Moose Lake. Looking at us, he took off his sunglasses, blasted his horn, twice, and was in front of Cozy Shores by the time his boat wake covered our ankles and crashed against the pier posts. Heidi said, "Now that guy's a real catch."

"You know him?" I asked.

"I'd sure like to," she said.

Dan changed the subject. "Let's go to Louie's Landing for a cheeseburger." The four of us walked off the pier and to the boat dock, a stretch of narrow piers and wooden fishing boats covered by a tin roof. Dan stepped onto the stern seat of our rented row boat and said, "Give us a minute to tidy up." Two empty Sprite cans floated in a pool of water just deep enough to cover the wooden ribs at the bottom of the boat. He tossed the cans into a neighboring boat, grabbed an empty five-pound Maxwell House Coffee can, and scooped the standing water – six cans full – back into Moose Lake. I stepped onto the boat's middle seat, shoved our musky rods to one side, and stashed the huge landing net under the seat. While Dan checked the gas tank, I helped Tina onto the bow seat and Heidi onto the middle seat, next to me. Dan began his fore-play with the Evinrude, a temperamental, five-horse out-board which he had bought from his uncle and painted Fire Engine Red. With an oar, I shoved us out of our dock while Dan reared back on the starter rope, once, twice, thrice.

"Damn thing!" he said, looking at me.

Tina said, "It'll never start if you talk to it like that."

Dan said, "Oh, I get it." He turned to the Evinrude, put his hand across his heart, and said, "Sweetheart! Will you ever forgive me?"

"Choke her," I said.

"I did!" he said, his voice tone adding, shut up!

Heidi pointed at my Musky Buster – an orange plastic tackle box at our feet – and asked, "What's in there?" I opened it and pulled up three levels of plastic shelves lined with musky lures.

"Come on lovely!" Dan shouted as he choked and un-choked the engine between pulls.

I picked up a Cisco Kid, a fat black wooden plug as long as my hand and covered with silver sparkles, my favorite. Metal propellers were fastened to the Kid's nose and tail, and three huge treble hooks hung from its belly. When retrieved, the Kid churned and gurgled its way across the lake's surface like a small creature about to die. I held the Kid close to Heidi and said, "Look at these tooth marks!"

The Evinrude started, blowing out blue smoke, buzzing and rattling like a chain saw. A mound of bubbles broke the surface behind the outboard, as if we were about to fiercely accelerate, but we were not one man sitting in front of ninety race horses, we were four people sitting in front of five old nags. I yelled to Dan, "Is she wide open?"

He yelled back angrily, "What do you think?"

I turned to Heidi and said, "That musky hit this Kid at the side of the boat and all hell broke loose!" I didn't tell her that moments later that musky had spit my Kid into the air and dropped it between my feet, as if aimed. "A musky's got to be thirty inches to be a keeper. That musky was forty inches easy." It was a strain to talk above the buzz of the motor, so the four of us fell into our own thoughts and didn't speak. Hugging the shore, we rounded Piney Point, a little spit of land crowded with towering white pines. A bald eagle perched on a dead branch high in one of the pines and watched us pass below, its brilliant white head slowly turning to keep us in sight.

Twenty minutes later, Dan shut off the motor and we glided alongside the public pier at Louie's. Heidi said, "We could have walked and got here faster." We helped the girls out of the boat and walked towards Louie's, a white frame building with dark green roof and lots of windows. Inside, we sat side by side on chrome-legged barstools fitted with red and green boat cushions. A fifty-pound musky, the Moose Lake record, hung above the rows of brown and green liquor bottles behind the bar, its olive green body as thick as my waist and curled away from the wall, as if turning to face us. Its mouth was wide open and lined with yellow-dagger teeth.

Dan said, "I bet he could swallow a softball and not blink."

"He looks mean," Heidi said. While she looked at the

musky, I looked at that soft hollow spot where her chest and throat came together. We ordered cheeseburgers and cokes. I didn't know what to say to a girl who lived thirty stories in the air, but she was a such a talker that I didn't have to say much. "I go to an all-girls' high school," she said. "Graduate next year."

"Then what?" I asked, keeping the focus on her.

"I'll go to an all-boys' college." She smiled. I did not doubt her.

Back in our boat, Heidi and I sat closer together, our bare thighs so close that the hair on my thighs caught the static electricity from her skin and bristled. Tina sat next to Dan on the stern seat with nothing but the motor handle between them, which put the bow so high into the air that Dan had to look around the boat to see where he was going. When we came alongside Piney Point, he shut off the motor and the boat glided to a stop in the water, a hundred feet from shore.

"I'm going to swim across the lake," Dan announced. "Tina said she'd row ahead of me."

Heidi shook her head. "I wouldn't swim in this lake after seeing that musky at Louie's."

Dan laughed and said, "No problem!" He pulled off his tee-shirt, held his nose, and flipped over backwards into the water like Lloyd Bridges in Sea Hunt. The boat rocked. He came up, threw his head to the side to get his hair out of his eyes and said, "These wet shorts weigh a ton."

Tina said, "So take them off." Dan raised that right eyebrow again and sank out of sight. A moment later, his hand – clutching his shorts – broke the surface. When his head appeared, Heidi and Tina cheered like the home team had just scored in the last second of play. This confused me. I knew that men were supposed to hoot and holler when a woman took off her clothes, but I had never figured that this might also hold true when reversed. Dan brushed his wet bangs off his face, smiling. Tina pulled the musky net from underneath the seat and held it over the side of the boat like a basketball hoop. Dan balled up his wet cutoffs, tossed them into the net, and sank out of sight. His hand – clutching his white jockeys – broke the surface. When his head appeared, Tina yelled, "Danny boy!" as if she had known him for years. He tossed his jockeys into the air and a trail of water followed them into the musky net. Tina lifted the net into the boat like she had just landed a keeper.

Heidi looked at me and asked, "You afraid to swim across?" I pulled off my shirt and dove over the side of the boat into Moose Lake, Grade-A musky water. Staying under, I peeled off my cut-offs and jockeys, swam under the boat, and surfaced on the other side of the boat, near Dan. Heidi and Tina had their backs to me, searching the water for me. I balled up my clothes, tossed them, and they splattered against Heidi's back. She screamed, turned, and laughed.

Tina grabbed the oars and faced us, ready to escort our swim. Heidi sat with her back to us and took off her wet blouse, which revealed a white tube-top beneath her bare shoulders. Glancing over her shoulder to make sure we were both looking at her, Heidi pulled her tube-top over her head. Dan and I treaded water, silent, so stunned that we forgot to hoot and holler. Her hair fell across the white swimsuit line on her bare back. I thought, if her back is this beautiful, why … At that moment, Heidi pulled her legs across the seat, turned, and faced us, her hands folded across her breasts like the lingerie models in the J.C. Penny Catalog. My arms stopped moving, and I sank to my eyes, sucking in a noseful of water. Tina rowed. We swam. I coughed.

Out of the corner of his mouth, Dan said, "I got a boner you wouldn't believe."

"Tell me about it," I said.

Side by side, we swam a slow and easy breast-stroke, refusing to dip our heads under water at the end of each stroke for fear of missing the moment when Heidi might drop her arms to her sides or hold them out wide. Tina rowed toward the middle of the lake and we swam about thirty feet behind the boat. The water got colder, deeper. For a moment, I imagined the cousin of that musky at Louie's lying on the bottom – like a log with teeth – looking up at us. I thought, we must look like a pair of soft, pale Cisco Kids being trolled behind the boat. The stiff rudder between my legs pointed toward the depths below. I thought, if a musky could swallow a softball, why …

Dan yelled, "Oh my God! Yaaaa!" He stopped swimming and fearfully searched the water around his body.

"What's wrong?" I yelled.

"Something's going for me!" I knew instantly that a fifty-pound musky was circling him like a shark as he beat the water around him with his fists. I cupped my groin with one hand and swam a one-armed freestyle toward the boat. Dan and I reached opposite sides of the boat at the same time, heaved our bodies up and out of the water, tucked our shoulders, rolled, and landed on our butts, shoulder to shoulder, on the bottom of our boat. I looked up at Heidi, who already had on her tube-top and was pulling on her blouse. The girls had no idea why we had rushed the boat and now lay beneath them as naked as newborns. They must have thought that we were trying to pull a fast one because Heidi frowned, pointed at my crotch, and said angrily, "Cover that up right now!" I grabbed a boat cushion and covered myself. Dan did a cross-your-crotch with his hands. Heidi stood, looked across the lake, and waved her arms in the air. We didn't move. A boat horn blasted, twice, and a speedboat closed, slowed, and circled us, its engine gurgling water. A man's voice yelled, "You girls in trouble?"

Heidi pointed down at us and yelled, "Double trouble!"

Not knowing what to do, we stayed on our backs on the bottom of the boat. The man maneuvered his boat alongside our boat and bumped us, hard. He stood up, leaned over, took off his sunglasses, and nodded at us, as if we'd just been introduced at a party. He smiled and said to the girls, "They're hardly keepers! Why don't you throw them back!"

Heidi asked, "Can you take us to Cozy Shores?"

"At your service!" He reached out his hairy arm, escorted each girl from our boat onto his boat, backed away, blasted his horn, twice, cracked his whip, and brought his ninety horses to life. We didn't move. The power of that black Mercury rattled the wooden ribs of our boat and set our naked bodies vibrating. A moment later, the wake of his boat lifted us, lowered us, lifted us, lowered us.

MAY I BRING MY BRIDE?

Frederick stood at the bay window of his McKinley Street mansion, stroked his white beard, and watched the snow swirl and blow. He had not told his children about his wedding. How can I tell them? he had asked himself. They will not accept my bride so soon after their mother's passing. They will not accept my way of grief. Frederick wore a black suit, starched white shirt, and burgundy tie knotted in a windsor, the knot of a gentleman. He held his head like a young man, proud and ready, but Katherine's passing had taken something from his body, as if someone had knocked the wind out of him and he still clutched from the blow.

Two months earlier, Frederick had stood at the head of his wife's open grave, his ten grown children surrounding the grave like a wreath. The night of her burial, Katherine had come to Frederick in a dream, touched his trembling hand, said gently, "Whatever we did or did not have is over. You will not make it alone. You must marry." He had pulled his hand away from her but knew that she was right.

A fire crackled and hissed behind Frederick in the front-room fireplace. Hans, Frederick's houseservant for thirty years, held an iron poker in his white-gloved hand and stirred the logs. A 1928 Packard turned into the circle drive-way, running boards and fenders covered with road slush. Frederick turned to Hans and said, "The bride has arrived."

Frederick opened the double oak doors and welcomed Ida with a deep bow. She stood five feet tall and weighed ninety pounds, a lady, frail as lace, with the wrists and ankles of a bird – skin over bone – and thin silver hair. She wore a high-collar, black wool suit and wire spectacles. A heavy, big-nosed man escorted Ida, a longtime friend of Frederick's, a justice of the peace. Hans collected their coats and hats and Frederick stretched out his arm toward the front room and said, "Please, come warm yourselves by the fire."

Two weeks earlier, Hans had delivered Frederick's hand-written proposal to Ida, which read, "I have admired you since I first met you so many years ago. May I have your hand in holy matrimony?" Stunned, she had put her hand over her heart and said, "Tell him I must pray about this. Come back for my reply in a week." She had slept little that week and prayed for a sign. On the night before Hans was to return for her answer, she had looked out her bedroom window at the night sky and saw two stars so close together that they looked like one. Oh! she thought, how they ease one another's loneliness! William has been gone for five years. It is good that I marry again.

Side by side, Frederick and Ida stood on the blood-red Chinese rug in front of Frederick's fireplace, facing the justice and the leaping flames behind him. Ida's left hand rested on Frederick's raised right forearm and her right hand rested by her hip, clutching a lavender handkerchief. After the vows,

Frederick pulled a gold ring from his watch pocket and slid the ring up Ida's bony finger. The justice nodded to him and said, "You may now kiss the bride." Ida closed her eyes and turned her face toward Frederick, and he leaned down and kissed her on the cheek just as an oak knot exploded in the fireplace. Turning to Hans, he said, "You may now bring in Ida's trunk."

Frederick owned Cream City Doorbells, a thriving company which manufactured electric doorbells, the latest mark of status for American homeowners. Frederick's eldest son, Walter, worked as one of Frederick's salesman and even though Frederick had never mentioned it, Walter knew that one day he would run the company. To Walter, this meant ordering his life in a particular way: marrying well, attending the right church, joining Milwaukee Society – all of which he had accomplished, with style. His home had a Cream City doorbell at the front and back door.

The day after his wedding, Frederick invited Walter into his office toward the end of the day, for sales talk. The five o'clock factory whistle blew and Frederick pushed a gold-plated box of Cuban cigars across his desk toward his son, signaling an end to business. Walter took a cigar, rolled it under his nose, and lit it. He leaned back in the leather chair, unbuttoned his vest, and slipped a hand between his big belly and his wool slacks. "I went to Wanderer's Rest on Saturday," he said. "I can't believe Ma's gone."

"I believe it!" answered Frederick, sharply.

Surprised, Walter changed the subject. "Millie and I are going to check on the summer home on Saturday. Want to drive out with us?" Frederick had bought the Snail Lake home in 1898 as a summer retreat from city heat, a Queen Anne Victorian with eight bedrooms, summer kitchen, flush toilet and wood stove. A screened-in porch stretched across the entire front of the home and caught the slightest lake breeze like a sail. Frederick's children now brought their children to the summer home like Frederick and Katherine had once brought them.

Frederick did not know how to answer Walter's question. He stood, walked to his office window, and watched a black car drive away between the tall, dirty snowbanks on each side of the street. Turning to face his son, he said, "I'd like to see the summer home. May I bring my bride?"

Walter drove straight to his sister's house. Minnie was the eldest and best educated of Frederick's children, the one to whom they all turned for advice. Minnie had dedicated her life to her parents, brothers, and sisters, and to the third-graders at McKinley School, having escorted twenty classes through McGuffy's Reader, verse by verse. Worry lines crossed her forehead like rivers. Having no husband to turn to, she turned elsewhere for her strength and counsel. Her brothers and sisters had come to trust her tarot and ouija board readings, though she had never told Frederick where she got her strength, figuring he'd disapprove. After Katherine's burial, Minnie had gathered her brothers and sisters at her house, shuffled her tarot deck, and pulled one card, the four of wands, "Completion." Minnie nodded and said, "Mom is at peace."

Walter rang Minnie's Cream City doorbell furiously. When Minnie opened her door, Walter brushed by her into the front room and without taking off his wool overcoat he began to pace in front of her fireplace.

"What's gotten into you?" Minnie asked.

He raised his finger like an exclamation point and said, "She's after Pa's money!"

Confused, Minnie asked, "Who's after Pa's money?"

"Ida Betzendorf – his new wife, as of Saturday."

"Pa's retired bookkeeper?" Walter nodded. Minnie put her fingers over her mouth, closed the door and walked to the front-room window. Walter watched her, waiting for her reply. She shook her head but said nothing, which frustrated Walter.

"Pick a card," he said.

She sat in her stuffed, gold chair, pulled her tarot deck out of the crevice between the chair and seat cushion, and began to shuffle the cards. Suddenly, she stopped shuffling and turned over the top card. "The three of swords," she said. "Sorrow."

After Walter left, Minnie went to the wall phone, lifted the receiver and put it to her ear. She heard her neighbor's voice on the party line and said stiffly, "Mabel, you get off this phone right now. I got an emergency." Minnie rang up her four sisters, stunning each of them with the news of their father's wedding, and saying to each sister, "Stay away from her." When Walter got home, he told his wife and then rang up his four brothers, describing Ida as "a gold-digger."

Two weeks after the wedding, Frederick put a cut-glass decanter on his desk and ordered his secretary to keep it filled with brandy. Each day, just after the five o'clock whistle, he poured himself a tumbler of brandy and walked to his office window, swirling the liquor in his glass. It is as I feared, he thought. Walter can't look me in the eye. Minnie no longer phones.... Once, while lying in bed and unable to sleep, Ida turned her head toward Frederick and said, "Your children hate me." Frederick lay still.

"No. They hate me," he said. His hand slid over the feather-bed toward her but stopped short of her warm body. Frederick thought, the summer home will bring us all together. That winter, the snow stayed on the ground until April.

Minnie supervised spring cleaning at the summer home. She was the first to arrive that Memorial Day, the back seat of her car full of mops and buckets and brooms. She unlocked the back door and went from window to window, rapping the window frames with a wooden spoon, pulling them open. By the time Frederick's Dusenberg pulled up the gravel drive, Minnie and several of her sisters were gathered in the yard, beating the winter dust out of a rug. Frederick parked along-side Walter's car on the grass and shut off the engine. Ida looked at him, fear in her eyes, and said, "They don't want me here."

Frederick got out, walked around the car, opened her door and said, "This is your home too."

Ida took a deep breath as she walked up to her stepdaughters, who looked at her without speaking. Frederick said, "Perhaps Ida can give a hand here." He picked up a wire rug-beater and handed it to his wife. She walked stiffly to one side of the forest-green rug which hung over the clothesline. Minnie stood on the other side of the rug, watching Ida. Ida swung at the rug like an uncertain batter who half swings at a pitch. Minnie swung next, hard: Whap! Dust exploded toward Ida, who took a step back.

Frederick walked past the house and down the long hill to the lake. His five sons were working together at lake's edge, assembling the pier. Frederick took a hammer out of the tool box, walked onto the first section of pier and knelt next to Walter. Without looking at his father, Walter handed him a fistful of spikes and together they nailed the long planks to the cross beams. No one spoke because no one knew what to say.

Later, Frederick showed Ida their upstairs bedroom. Ida stood in the doorway and watched her husband check the mattresses and dresser drawers for mouse nests. She noticed a painting of Katherine on the oversized dresser. Frederick walked to the dresser and put the portrait into the top drawer, face down. "I'm sorry," he said. "I haven't been in this room since her death."

Minnie appeared at their bedroom door and with a forced politeness asked, "Will you two be staying for dinner?"

Ida said, "We have to be going, thank you."

At dinner, Walter told Minnie, "Pa ain't saying so, but he's mad at us. He could kick us all out of here."

On the drive back to her new McKinley Street home, Ida held her lavender handkerchief against her face with both hands. Frederick pulled his car onto the grass shoulder, stopped, and laid his hand on Ida's shoulder, the first time he had touched her since the wedding. "I'll ask them to leave," he said. "They were unkind to both of us."

Ida dropped her hands and looked at her husband. She saw how much he wanted to make things better for her. He saw how lovely she looked with tears swelling in her eyes. "You can't ask them to leave," she said. "They belong there. I don't."

"I won't ask you to go there again," he said. Frederick put his hands back on the steering wheel and pulled onto the gravel highway. He knew then that the summer home would not bring them together, that he had to find another way forward for his family.

On Flag Day, Frederick drove to the summer home, alone. He rang the Cream City doorbell and waited at the screen door, as if a guest. Minnie came to the door. Startled to see her father, she looked for Ida. Frederick said, "I'm alone. Tell your brothers and sisters to meet me on the porch – immediately." Minnie had not heard him use that word with her since she was a girl. One by one, his children, like bewildered cattle chased in from pasture, appeared on the porch: Walter, Minnie, Freddie, Harry, Bill, Lidia, Lily, Katie, John, Bessie.

Frederick asked his children to find a seat and he sat in his favorite wicker rocker. "I have an announcement," he said, without anger. "It's clear to me that Ida is not welcome here. I do not go where my wife is not welcome." His children glanced at one another, ashamed of their anger but unable to abandon it. "I have always intended to give you this place at the time of my death, but I have changed my mind." Walter thought, here it comes! Ida gets the summer home! Frederick said, "I give it to you now, rather than later." Walter's eyes widened, and he glanced at Minnie. Frederick pointed to the cottage next door and said, "I bought Riley's place last week. Ida and I will make our home there on weekends. You may visit us anytime." Satisfied, Frederick got up and walked off the porch. His children sat in their wicker chairs, silent, blinking heavily, staring at his empty chair, which hadn't finished rocking.

Ida and Frederick moved into the Riley cottage that next weekend. Frederick's children did not visit them but did take turns watching Frederick and Ida from behind the lace curtain at the top of the stairs. At dinner time, the conversation revolved around what Ida did or did not do that day. Minnie scooped some mashed potatoes onto her plate and said, "That woman planted geraniums by the back door where's there's not enough sun to grow a fern."

That next Saturday morning, Ida and Frederick sat on the wooden bench at the end of their pier and watched the sailboat races across the lake. Ida's head dropped to her chest and her body slumped against Frederick. He shook her by the shoulders. "Ida! Oh my God! Help!" Her sun bonnet slipped off her head, rolled on its brim across the pier and into the water. Walter heard his father's yell and ran across the wooded lot, onto their pier, and gathered Ida in his arms. He carried her off the pier, her bent legs swinging free in his arms, and laid her on the grass under the shade of a shoreline hickory. Walter lifted her wrist and felt for a pulse. He looked at his father, who knelt next to Ida, held her other hand, and looked across the lake, as if he were trying to see something far off in the distance. Ida's bonnet floated like a lily on the water.

Ida's wake was held at Frederick's McKinley Street home. Hans dressed Ida in her wedding suit, and folded her hands over her chest, tucking a lavender handkerchief in between her hip and the side of the coffin. She lay in the parlor, the coolest room of the house, where Katherine's body had laid in state seven months earlier. Frederick's children came to the wake in their finest black clothes. Minnie arrived early and helped Hans serve coffee and tea. She was the only one of Frederick's children to go into the parlor and look at Ida, and her face flushed with shame and guilt. Walter stood on the porch and greeted arriving mourners, most of whom were Frederick's employees. That evening, the house quiet and dark, Frederick stood alongside Ida's coffin. He bent forward, closed his eyes and pressed his lips against her cheek, slowly, letting his lips feel her cold skin. He buried Ida next to Katherine, with room enough between his two wives for his own grave.

Frederick rented out the Riley cottage and moved back into the upstairs bedroom he had shared with Katherine. His first night back in the summer home was not ordinary. At midnight, a loud *knock! knock! knock!* echoed through the home, as if someone were rapping a cane against a wood wall. Walter awakened and raised himself to his elbows for a better listen. It's coming from downstairs! he thought. Minnie lay in bed with her eyes open and thought, it's coming from upstairs! *Knock! Knock! Knock!*

At the breakfast table, Walter asked, "Did anyone hear that knocking last night?" Frederick's children nodded. No one else did. Frederick looked up from his oatmeal and asked, "What knocking?" Night after night, the knocking continued and only Frederick's children heard it.

Late one night, after Frederick and his grandchildren and in-laws had gone to bed, Frederick's ten children gathered on the porch to plan Frederick's July-tenth birthday supper, by tradition prepared by his sons in the summer kitchen, and by tradition: corn on the cob, steaks, green beans, pancakes with great globs of butter, pear kuchen.

Knock! Knock! Knock! Knock!

Walter looked at the ceiling and raised his fist. "If you have something to say to us why don't you say it in English, like a man!" Everyone looked at Minnie, since this was her territory, but she did not speak.

At midnight that next evening, Minnie set up a card table on the porch and put a storm candle on one corner. She reached under the wicker couch and placed her ouija board on the table. With only the candle for light, Minnie and Walter sat down across from one another, the board between them, their four brothers and four sisters standing around them, shoulder to shoulder, like wolves around a kill. Minnie said, "Our question will be: What is this knocking trying to tell us?" Walter had not used a ouija board since he was a boy, but he remembered what to do. He and Minnie lightly placed their fingertips on the wooden marker and let it move freely across the board, like a raft floating free on a lake. When it stopped moving, Minnie checked to see which letter of the alphabet it pointed toward. First came an *i*, then an *n*, then the rest of the letters, *v, i, t, e, m, e.* Minnie said, "That's all, that's the whole message: *Invite me.*"

An owl hooted down by the lakeshore and Walter felt the hair on the back of his neck rise. "Invite who to what?" he asked.

Minnie looked at the faces of her brothers and sisters in the flickering candlelight. "This message is from Ida," she said. They gasped and took a step back.

"How do you know?" asked Walter.

"I just know."

Walter said, "The damn woman makes more noise dead

than alive! And why does she knock like that? We're a door-bell family! We make doorbells! We ring doorbells! We don't knock!"

Minnie added, "I know how we can stop the knocking."

On July tenth, the men worked in the summer kitchen and the women, each holding a tall glass of lemonade, gathered on the pier. At noon, Walter rang the dinner bell and soon each member of the family stood behind his or her chair, waiting for Frederick's prayer. He folded his hands and prayed, in German: "Komm Herr Jesus, sei unser Gast, und segne was du aus deine Gnaden besheret hast. Amen." He opened his eyes, nodded, and everyone sat. Frederick looked at the opposite end of the thirty-foot table, where Katherine used to sit. Her place had been empty since her death, but for this occasion someone had set a full table service at her place. Confused, Frederick asked, "Are we missing someone?"

Walter took this as his cue. He pushed back his chair, stood, and waited for everyone to quiet down. "That's reserved for Mrs. Betzendorf – for Ida." Frederick looked at Walter as if his son had run him through with a sword. Walter continued, "I've been asked to offer a toast on behalf of my brothers." He turned to the empty chair and lifted his glass of ice water. "Ida, we welcome you to our table. Better late than never."

Walter's brothers lifted their glasses of ice water toward the empty chair and said in unison, "Here! Here!" Frederick's in-laws and grandchildren looked at one another, confused.

Walter added, "And praise God for America's finest door-bell, the Upstairs/Downstairs, our best model."

Again, "Here! Here!"

Walter sat and Minnie stood. "Ida. On behalf of my sisters,

I'm glad you didn't take no for an answer." She lifted her glass and was joined by her sisters. The grandchildren stared at the empty chair, expecting Ida's ghost to appear.

Frederick pushed back his chair and stood, slowly, as if it took all of his might to get to his feet. He looked at Walter and Minnie and each of his children. He looked at the empty chair at the other end of the table and bowed deeply, like he had when he had first welcomed Ida to his McKinley Street home the day of their wedding. The doorbell at the front door, the Upstairs/Downstairs, rang out like a church bell and startled everyone at the table. Frederick lifted his glass, a toast to Ida and his loved ones, living and dead. Ice water spilled over his trembling hand and onto the white table cloth.

LAST OF HIS KIND

WHEN I WAS A KID, wolves was our neighbors, and I ain't talking yippy little brush wolves, I'm talking timber wolves, the kind a wolf makes the hairs on your neck stand up and dance when he howls at the moon. At thirty below, I heared them howl on Otter Lake Ridge, four miles north of that little cabin I was born in. Ma was a Chippewa, grew up on Bad River. She knowed wolves better than she knowed people and told me, "I howled with the pain of you being born and a wolf howled back at me from across the lake. I took this as a good sign."

When I growed big enough, I helped Pa run his trapline. Pa and me caught mostly beaver, otter, marten, mink, and muskrat, couple lynx, three-four wolf, left plenty animals for seed. In spring, we took our pelts into town to see Sam Goldsmith, a Milwaukee fur-buyer who went town to town for pelts – first Jew I ever laid my eyes on up north. Sam gave us cash for fur and we bought what we couldn't make or grow – sugar, flour, oats, traps, rifles, whiskey – Irish whiskey. Dad drank only Irish whiskey and growed his own potatoes in a little clearing near our cabin, said it was bad luck for a full blood

Irishman to eat a potato he hadn't growed hisself. He loved to hear them wolves at night, said they sounded Irish to him.

Things got bad after Pa died. The Depression hit us and the logging shut down, which dried up the pine money. Lots of men went after wolf money and nobody blamed them – hell, a wolf skin brought twenty bucks, another twenty for bounty – good money when you figure they was making twenty cents an hour working the big pines. Some of them loggers had shoulders big as tree trunks from swinging an axe ten hours a day! I had to support a wife and kid and my ma in them years, so like the rest, I got greedy. Took twenty wolf one winter, got a name in my parts for wolf trapping. The game warden asked me to trap wolves for the State but I said, "Hell no. I don't take State wages for killing."

After the war, the veterans came back, got married, built their cabins, got drunk, and shot whatever moved in the woods. Got shot myself, in the arm by a kid from town, said I looked like a deer to him. Drunk! Buck fever hit the cities and the woods began to fill up with city men who didn't know a wolf from a fox, but when they didn't get their buck, they said, "It's the wolves. They're killing all our deer. The only good wolf is a dead wolf." I'd sit on my porch on the night of the full moon and listen, but all I heared was brush wolves and owls, no more wolves.

Maybe ten years later, I ran into Bill Hogan one winter day where our traplines crossed by Pine Lake. He says, "I seen wolf tracks, one wolf. I'll get him before you." I laughed at him and said, "Got to be a brush wolf, Bill. No wolves left." A week later, he pulls a toe out of his pocket and says, "I had him but he twisted out, left this." I still didn't believe him till

I saw wolf tracks for myself, one wolf. Bill hadn't been the first to get him in a trap. He was missing plenty of toes on both front paws. Each night, I listened for him but I never heared him howl, never seen another track. Word got around about that wolf. Next thing I knowed he's in the news, "Old Two Toes, Last Wolf in Wisconsin." That's when I made up my mind to get him.

I knowed Old Two Toes was trapwise so I figured, I got to fool him. I looked at the wolf traps hanging in my shed: Victor Newhouse number-threes and fours, a few with teeth, big traps, hard to hide. I left them hanging and got half dozen of my strongest number-two double longsprings, fox traps, smaller, easier to hide. I reboiled them in bark water along with chains and two-hooked drags and hung my fur coat outside where the wind could blow away my smell.

I didn't know where that wolf was but I knowed where the wolves used to run, so I put out six sets with those fox traps, three baited, three blind, careful not to leave any scent. I checked them sets each day, along with the my sets for beaver and otter and mink. Got a brush wolf the first night, a red fox the night after. After the third night, I came up to my blind set between the swamp and ridge and seen that my trap was gone, dragged off into the cedars, trees twice as thick as my finger bit in two along the way. Then I seen him ahead of me, a big male, black as coal, all tangled up in a root pile, fighting like hell to get out of that little fox trap! When he seen me, he changed. He give up, lie down like a dog, staring at me with them greenfire eyes I hadn't seen in twenty years.

I took my hatchet out of my pack and walked up to him, ready to clip, hang, and cut him. He didn't move, didn't flatten his ears against his skull, didn't whine or growl or blink. Wolves is too proud for all that, and besides, they're smart enough to know when they're licked. I surprised myself and sat down this far from him. He was old, gray like me on his face and chest, skin and bones, maybe eighty pounds, hundred twenty in his prime. I had him by two toes on his hind leg. I started talking to him like he's a long lost friend, "I bet you used to run at the head of your pack and howl all night." It started to snow. Big white flakes fell onto his black fur and did not melt. I said, "Now you run the woods alone, quiet as this falling snow." The greenfire burned in his eyes but he did not move.

"You and me," I said, "We're the last of our kind." God save me, I thought. I slowly reached for the trap. He showed his teeth – worn and yellow as mine, but he didn't go for me. I grabbed both trap springs, clamped down, and pulled the trap off his toes. Boom! Up he comes like a shot, off he goes, so shook up to be free again that he ran right into a cedar trunk and damn near killed hisself. Bill Hogan never caught that wolf, and he never believed me when I told him that I caught Old Two Toes and let him go.

Later that winter, someone gave me a copy of that little paper out of Bayfield, dated January 26, 1958, half a year after the wolf bounty was lifted by the State. There was this story in that paper, an interview with a damn Swede named Ogren, a banker no less, Willard Ogren. He told about how he was driving his '56 Buick on County C between Bayfield and Cornucopia. He seen what he thought was a dog in the road ahead, running away from his car. He says the road was snow-slick and that he was doing sixty-five so he couldn't stop. Bam! He got the car stopped about a block down the road and he and his banker friend walked back and seen that they hit a wolf, a black wolf, and that the wolf's back was broke but he wasn't dead. Ogren clubbed the wolf dead with his tire iron and put him on top of his trunk. On the way to town, the wolf got up and jumped off his car. Ha! Old Two Toes had other plans for how he wanted to die. Ogren stopped, clubbed him again, put him back on his trunk, drove to Grandish's restaurant, got a knife, and slit his throat. Hell, if I knowed ahead of time that Old Two Toes was going to die on top of a Swedish banker's Buick, I'd have done him a favor and killed him in the woods when I had him.

Now he's gone and there's just me.

GIDDUP!

A BLOOD-RED, BLACK-MASKED CARDINAL gripped a branch high above Franz and sang to the bare woods, "Cheer! Cheer! Cheer!" Franz took off his coat, tossed it over a cedar branch, and thought, what a day to work the woods – spring in January! He wrapped the logging chain around the felled birch, stepped back, and looked at Prince, his work horse, a blond-and-brown Belgian which stood seventeen hands at the shoulder, weighed eighteen hundred pounds, and worked out of pleasure, like Franz. Franz shouted, "Giddup!" Prince snorted, hit it, and skidded the tree out of the elderbrush thicket, gouging last year's leaves and black earth onto the snow. Without warning, two limbs from the skidding birch struck Franz from behind and slammed him into the cedar. He shouted "Whoa!" and Prince stopped. Dazed, Franz grabbed the cedar trunk to keep from falling. He thought, something's wrong, but what? He looked down at his left leg. A bone stuck out of his jeans, just above the knee, and the leg swelled like a tire being filled with air. Blood darkened his pants.

No pain. Just the thought, you done it this time Franz!

Snapped off your leg in the swamp – alone! His good leg gave out and he went down, rolling onto his back as the pain hit. He clenched his teeth and told himself, take it! Take the pain! There's nothing else you can do! A second wave of pain hit and he passed out.

An hour later, Franz came to. His leg throbbed, but less. His first thought, the bleeding must have stopped or I'd be dead by now. Melted snow soaked the back of his red-and-black plaid shirt. Prince snorted. Franz rolled his head and looked at his horse, which had not moved since Franz's last command and would not move until he received another. Prince swung his head around and looked at his fallen master. Franz studied his horse's huge face, blond bangs dangling across a white forehead, eyes like ripe plums, unblinking.

Afraid to look at his leg again, Franz thought about his predicament. If I move too much I'll bleed again sure as hell – or go into shock. Thank God it ain't colder than it is! Franz lifted his head off the snow, took off his red wool cap and pulled down the ear flaps, one small thing he could do to keep warm. He pulled his cap over his head, snugly, and said to Prince, "Dad said he would check on us this afternoon. We'll sit tight and wait for him."

Franz lived alone, a bachelor at forty, a loner all his life. As a boy, he had spent more time with farm animals than friends. At lambing time, he had insisted on sleeping in the barn, wrapped in an old quilt, one end of a string tied to his finger, the other end tied to the leg of a ewe ready to lamb. When the ewe moved, she tugged Franz's finger, awakening him, bringing him to her side. He had spent hours each week grooming his dad's team of Belgians, standing on a ladder to brush their manes and rumps. His dad had once remarked to his mom, "Mama, the boy loves them horses more than girls! What are we to do with him?" Just after Franz moved onto his own farm, his dad had said, "Son, you get lonely you get yourself a wife." Franz had smiled and said, "I ain't the type to marry, Dad." Most evenings, Franz returned to his boyhood home and ate dinner with his parents. The three ate in silence, like the animals in the barn.

During the week, Franz repaired phone lines from the tops of swaying cedar poles, a tree-top view of the forests and farms he loved. The skin on his face and hands looked like leather from years of wind, sun, and cold. In his free time, Franz tended a dozen head of beef, thirty sheep, and twenty acres of corn and alfalfa. He worked his fields with Prince and horse-drawn machinery, proud he did not own a tractor. Each Saturday after the swamp had frozen, he worked Prince, logging in the old way, like his dad had taught him.

Franz's house had been built for a big farm family. He painted the outside of the house every three years and tended the yard weekly, but he neglected the inside of the house in a way which was obvious even from the road – torn, yellowed shades, many half-pulled down, hung behind each window. He had closed off the entire upstairs and used only the kitchen, living room, and bathroom, though he preferred the outhouse, where he stapled Playboy centerfolds to the back of the door. Franz ate his breakfasts in the living room – on a T.V. tray – and slept on a sagging, forest-green couch. Piles of yellowed newspapers and dated issues of *Draft Horse Journal* leaned against the back of the couch. If a neighbor came by, Franz stepped onto the porch and visited with them there, even at twenty below. Few people got inside his house or his life.

Trying to keep his mind off his injury, Franz spoke to Prince. "As soon as your Mama dropped you, Dad called me. I saw you stand for the first time. You was all legs. I told Dad right then, 'I want him.' Every day after work I sat by you, ran my hands up and down your legs so you'd get used to me. Hell, I could pick you up with one arm then!" He smiled. "Now look at you – a crane couldn't lift you!" Franz thought about his leg again and fell silent. The bare crowns of the trees crisscrossed the blue sky above him like a spider web. A black raven flew over him, high and alone: "Caw! Caw! Caw!"

Think about Dad, he told himself. He closed his eyes and imagined his father walking down the logging trail, sensing trouble, running to him, kneeling beside him, his Dad's fine face looking down at him like it used to from the edge of his bed.

Come and get me Dad....

Come and get me Dad....

Come and get me Dad.... He sent this thought between the trees and over the frozen land like a telephone line.

Sometime in the middle of the afternoon, his mind still fixed on his father, he heard, far away, a girl laugh and a dog bark. He thought, that'll be Joanne and her collie. Franz took a deep breath and yelled to his eight-year-old neighbor, "Help!" The swamp echoed his cry, and a flock of chickadees in the cedar above him fluttered away. He closed his eyes and imagined Joanne throwing a red ball across her front yard, her collie in chase. How pretty she is! he thought. When I see her again, I'll throw the ball with her. "Help!" he yelled again. Joanne paused from her play and looked toward the swamp.

Franz thought about Joanne's father, Dennis, who had no use for horses. Last March, after bogging his tractor in the mud, Dennis had phoned Franz and said, "My tractor's up to the axles. Let's see what your horse can do." Franz had harnessed Prince, led him across the muddy field, and chained him to the John Deere bumper. He had looked at Dennis, smiled, and teased, "Nothing runs like a Deere, huh?" Franz had yelled, "Giddup!" and Prince had hit it, but the tractor hadn't budged. Dennis had said, "That horse ain't worth a shit!" Prince had taken a step back, snorted and hit it again, his dinnerplate-sized hooves tossing clods of mud against the tractor's grill, the tires beginning to roll. Franz had laughed out loud – a rare event – wrung his hands with pride, and said, "They say a Percheron can outpull a Belgian but they never seen my Prince!"

Franz listened for Joanne again, but because of a slight wind-shift could no longer hear her. That's when the cold hit him and his body clenched as if hit by electrical current. He looked at his coat on the branch above him and thought, might as well be in China! Franz rolled his head to the left and looked at the paling sun just above the dark green cedars. He thought, my God! It'll be dark soon. Where are you Dad? Tree shadows darkened and stretched across the snow.

The sky turned pink and the sun dropped behind the cedars, which now looked black. Franz's teeth began to chatter so violently that he thought they might crack and fall apart in his mouth. His mind shifted suddenly: he imagined himself sitting on the barn roof, surveying his farm. A woman he did not know came out of his house, stood on his porch, and waved at him. My God! he thought, that's my wife! This startled him – he had not dated a woman since high school and knew no woman who might want to marry him, but he felt an unexpected warmth radiate from his belly and quiet his shivers. Franz took a deep breath and looked at Prince, now a dark shape against the trees. The Belgian lifted a hoof, shifted his weight.

"Giddup!" Franz shouted.

Startled, Prince jerked his whole body and swung his head around, as if to check Franz's command.

"Giddup I said!"

Prince snorted, tensed.

"Giddup God Damn It!"

Prince hit it. The felled birch skidded past Franz and he listened to the crashing of horse and log through the swamp brush. When the crashing diminished, Franz knew that Prince was on the logging trail. When the swamp quieted, he knew that Prince stood beside the log pile at the edge of the swamp, blowing, waiting to be unchained from the log.

"Giddup!" he yelled again.

Prince, unaccustomed to far-off commands, turned his head toward Franz's voice but did not move.

"Giddup!"

Franz hoped that Prince would obey his command and pull to the barn. There, he figured, Dad or Dennis will see him. Prince hit it but did not pull toward the barn. He pulled straight across the pasture at a slow walk, head bobbing with each step, the tree gouging half-frozen sod. Prince reached the wood-and-wire snow fence which paralleled the road, stopped, and blew.

"Giddup!" Franz's voice, faraway but clear. The Belgian held his breath and turned his head toward the swamp, now a quarter mile behind him. Prince walked into the snow fence. His chest and legs pressed the fence to the ground, and the wood slats cracked and splintered under his front hooves. His body crossed the downed fence but the butt of the birch skidded under the fence and caught, halting the horse. Prince set his legs, dropped his hindquarters for extra power, and muscled ahead. The nearest metal stakes bent and pulled free of the frozen ground, and forty feet of the fence stretched toward the road like a bow bending with an archer's draw. The fence stretched only so far and halted Prince again. He paused and blew.

A great horned owl glided into Franz's view and landed on a birch branch above him. He looked at the huge bird silhouetted against the darkening sky, and the owl looked down at him. Franz lifted his arms and flapped them like wings. The owl opened its wings, stepped off the branch and glided off between the cedars without a sound. Franz returned to his imagined wife, and he followed her around his farmhouse: pale yellow curtains hung in kitchen windows. In his bedroom: a queen-size bed, his and her dressers, a full-length mirror. Never before had he been able to imagine a woman in his house, his life. Joy rose from his belly like a wave, warming him, lifting his loneliness.

"Giddup!" Franz yelled, straining.

Prince snorted and hit it. The fence held. He hit it, backed off, hit it, backed off, as he was taught to do with heavy logs, though there never was a log that had held him back more

116

than twice. Prince angled his line of pull and hit it again. The fence held but the butt of the tree broke free and sprang forward like a released arrow. Prince's body lurched ahead of his legs and his chest hit the frozen ground, heavily. The butt of the tree came down on Prince's outstretched hind leg and pinned it to the ground. He pulled his leg from under the log, tearing off a strip of hide. Putting out his front legs, he jerked himself to all fours and shook his head, dazed.

Franz imagined leading his wife into his bedroom. He pulled down the shades, sat on the bed, watched her undress.

Prince pulled toward the road, favoring his bad leg. The tugs and tree straightened out behind him as walked onto the asphalt, clip-clop, clip-clop, clip-clop. His belly above the white center line, Prince stopped, blocking both lanes with his body and the trunk of the tree. He shifted his weight off his bad leg and waited. Moonlight shone off his wide back.

Franz's father phoned his son for a third time, wondering why Franz had missed dinner. After five rings, he hung up and said, "Mama, something ain't right." He got into his pickup and drove toward Franz's place on the county road which connected their farms. Prince's eyes glowed like green coals in his headlights.

Franz swung his twenty-pound leg cast out of his pickup, got his crutches under his arms, and stood on his property for the first time since the accident, nine weeks earlier. He looked at his house, barn, sheds, then across the pasture toward the swamp, remembering the shouts of the men who had rescued him and the wrenching night ride out of the swamp on a snowmobile sled. A red-tailed hawk glided without sound five hundred feet above the swamp, circling to catch the updrafts where the woods met the field.

A mud-splattered, blue pickup turned into Franz's drive and pulled up next to Franz. Franz's neighbor, Dennis, shut off his truck, rolled down his window, lit a cigarette, and looked at Franz. "How's that leg of yours?"

Franz said, "I got more steel in this leg than you got on that truck." The men laughed, happy to see each other, and Franz added, "Place looks good. Thanks for taking care of it while I was laid up."

"You'd have done the same for me."

"How's Prince?"

"Got him in my barn. He's in good shape but restless as hell – wants to work again. Get in. See for yourself."

Dennis drove Franz to his farm and parked alongside the barn, which had all of the wooden doors and windows braced open to let in air and light. Franz got out of the truck and whistled, twice. He heard Prince snort in the barn and a moment later the horse put his head through an open window and watched the men walk toward him. Franz laid his crutches against the fieldstone wall and rubbed his cheek against Prince's wide, velvet nose, and Prince blasted his hot breath down the front of Franz's shirt.

Dennis said, "He's a good horse. I'd give you four thousand for him."

Startled by this offer, Franz said, "Not so long ago you told me Prince wasn't worth a shit!"

"Maybe I was wrong."

At supper that evening, Franz told his parents, "Dennis

offered four thousand for Prince, if that don't beat all."

"That's more than fair," answered his dad.

Frowning, Franz said, "Prince ain't for sale."

"Prince is ten. If you're ever going to sell him, this is your last chance to get a good price. I'll give you Danny Boy. He's ready to work."

Franz's mom added, "You owe Dennis something for looking after your place."

"Mom – Dennis knows tractors, not horses."

The phone rang and his mother answered it, nodded, looked at Franz, and said, "It's for you. A woman, mind you." Franz raised his eyebrows, stood, and said, "I'll get it in my room."

Franz made his way down the hall and into his boyhood room, which his mother had redone as a guest room when he had left – the walls now covered with pink wallpaper and his bed, dresser, chair, and nightstand painted with high-gloss black enamel. He leaned his crutches against the bed, picked up the phone, and said, "Hello?"

"Franz?"

"Ya."

"This is Lois, the second-shift nurse who took care of you."

"Oh ya." His hands began to tremble. He had not forgotten her, her plain, kind face, her strong hands.

"How you doing?"

"Not bad." During his first week in the hospital, he had said little to Lois, watching her as she tended him. His silence somehow brought her out and she found herself talking to him more as a friend than a patient, telling him about her mother, who had died a year earlier, and her sister, a nurse in

Milwaukee. She had also asked Franz about his life and learned about his parents, his farm, his neatly stacked wood-piles, and his way of climbing telephone poles and working horses.

Lois asked, "Are you still staying at your folks then?"

"Ya. Till I get this cast off. Then I'll move back to my place." A little round mirror hung on the wall across from him and in it he saw his face: a boy's eyes, bright, full of fear and joy; a man's look, tough, hidden. He pressed the black receiver hard against his ear and said, "Thanks for all you done for me."

"Let me know when you're coming to Green Bay again. We can have coffee."

Two days later, Franz drove past his farm on his way into town and was astonished to see Prince fully harnessed and pulling the manure spreader across Franz's alfalfa field. Dennis bobbed up and down on the spreader's spring metal seat, reins in hand, working Prince in a rough but competent way. Franz thought, I could teach him a thing or two, but he ain't doing half bad. He thought again about selling his horse to Dennis, knowing that Prince was turning the corner as a working horse and in a couple of years would be too old to do heavy work like logging. He also liked the idea of breaking in Danny Boy. That evening, he phoned Dennis and said, "Four thousand and he's yours. I'll throw in some training."

Dennis asked, "For Prince?"

"No. For you."

By late April, Franz was back on his farm, though still on disability with the phone company. On the morning of May Day, Franz took down his yellowed, torn window-shades and replaced them with new, white shades, which gave his home a very different look from the road. After lunch, he phoned Lois and said, "I got to go to Green Bay on Tuesday to see Doctor Hoch. Can you meet me for a cup of coffee in the hospital cafeteria?"

"Yes. I'd like that."

At four o'clock, Franz drove down the county road toward his folks, the road Prince had blocked with his body the night of Franz's accident. Franz looked to his left and saw Prince, hitched to an overloaded manure wagon which had bogged down in one of Dennis' muddy farm lanes. Dennis and his daughter, Joanne – red ball in her lap – sat on the spreader seat. Dennis cracked the reins above Prince's back and Prince hit it, backed off, hit it, backed off.

Franz stopped his truck, walked across the road, lifted his injured leg over the barbed-wire fence, and limped across the field as fast as he could, eager to calm Prince and assist Dennis, but before Franz got close, Dennis took out a leather whip and laid it across Prince's rump. Terrified, Prince flattened his ears against his skull, bulged his eyes, and hit it again and again, wildly. Franz got to Dennis unnoticed just as Dennis raised the whip a second time, and he pulled Dennis off the spreader and onto his back in the mud, jerking the whip out of his neighbor's hand. Stunned, Dennis looked up at Franz, who said with quiet fury, "Don't ever whip this horse again."

Franz looked at Joanne, who clutched her ball and stared at him, frightened. He looked back at Dennis and spoke with less fury and more grief. "I'm sorry." Franz offered his neighbor a hand, but Dennis stood without taking the offering.

"Dennis – Prince pulls out of pleasure, not fear."

"He's my horse now."

"I'll give you five thousand for him."

"He ain't for sale."

"Seven thousand."

"Just get my rig out of the mud."

Franz walked to Prince, calmed the horse with strokes and soft talk, and got on the spreader seat. "Giddup!" Prince set his hind legs, snorted, and hit it, and the wagon rolled forward, out of the mud.

At his folk's home, Franz threw the whip on the dining-room table and knocked over a vase of red tulips. The water from the vase dripped onto the carpet while Franz explained what had happened. Franz's father, upset now too, said, "I'll have a word with Dennis next time I see him."

On Tuesday morning, Franz finished his chores early and though he preferred showers, he took a bath, his first since he was a boy. He spent a long time looking at himself in the bathroom mirror, naked, combing his hair, brushing his teeth, putting on his blue dress-shirt, thinking about Lois and what he might say to her.

Franz got in his pickup and drove down the county road, slowly, past Dennis' barn, past Prince. The horse stood in a small corral, motionless, facing Franz's farm. Perched lightly on a roadside fencepost, a bluebird sang fiercely for its mate.

A MATCH MADE IN HEAVEN

MANNY LOOSENED his red polyester tie and reached inside his navy blue suitcoat for his gold retirement pen. His wife, Gladys, set a cup of Sanka and a sheet of her peach stationary on the kitchen table in front of him. Manny wrote:

> *Dear Bishop Stone,*
> *I just got back from ushering at Mildred Hoppel's funeral, bless her soul. She was our last charter member. There's only seventy of us Calvary Church folk left. Most of us ain't far behind Mildred.*
> *When them coloreds moved into our neighborhood we let them know they was welcome, just make it up those front steps which I admit are pretty steep and you'll get a free bible, we said, with the words of Jesus in red. They kept walking by as if we wasn't there.*
> *Our Reverend Morgan is retiring in June. He's done the best he can with what God gave him. He gave Mildred a good send off.*
> *We got to get some new blood in here or the doors will close for good.*

Manny had expected to close his letter with "Sincerely Yours," but he felt so inspired that he wrote,

In God's Service,
Manny Schaefer, Head Usher
Calvary United Methodist Church.

He folded the letter precisely, sealed it in a peach envelope, and walked it to the Burleigh Street post office. The stiff May breeze blew his tie across his shoulder like a scarf.

Two weeks later, Gladys gently shook Manny's shoulder. He opened his eyes and blinked. "It's the call you've been waiting for," she said.

"Never heard it ring," he said, pushing himself out of his La-Z-Boy and walking to the kitchen phone.

"Manny, this is Reverend Stiffler, Milwaukee District Superintendent. Bishop Stone has chosen your new pastor."

"Fine. Fine."

"Will you call a committee meeting for Wednesday at eight?"

"Yes. Wednesday at eight."

"You'll meet her then."

"Fine. Good day then, Reverend Stiffler." He put down the black receiver and sat across from Gladys at the kitchen table. "It's come to this," he said.

"Come to what?" Gladys asked.

"A woman."

Gladys thought about this a long while before asking, "What was in that letter you wrote?" Manny looked at the kitchen table as if his letter still lay before him and tried to remember his exact words.

That night, Manny lay beside Gladys, his hands behind his head, his eyes open, looking into the dark. He recalled, one by one, all of the pastors who had served Calvary, and he lined up their faces on his bedroom ceiling: all men, like Jesus. Once, a guest pastor – a woman nine-months pregnant – had preached at Calvary while Reverend Morgan was sunning himself in Florida. Since it was just after Christmas, she had spoken about the Virgin Birth, saying, "Whenever new life is birthed by God, that birth is Virgin, untouched by human will." As Head Usher, Manny hadn't heard much of her sermon because he was planning what he would do if her water broke before her sermon. Gladys, also awake, startled Manny when she spoke: "Maybe a woman can do what all those men never could."

That next morning, Manny phoned the committee members to tell them of the Wednesday meeting. At the end of each conversation, he added, as if a casual afterthought, "It ain't a him. It's a her."

John, the eldest at ninety-three, yelled into the phone, "Holy God, man! What kind of letter did you write our bishop?"

Manny reacted, "I didn't ask for no woman and you know it, so don't go telling people I did!"

Everybody showed for the meeting: six men, two women, all older than Manny. They gathered in the Adult Room, an interior room used for bible study, and, because it had no windows, for counting the weekly collection after worship. Manny's brass collection-plates were stacked under a large oil painting of Jesus, a Mildred Hoppel original. Jesus was dressed in a powder blue robe, his skin a pale beige. He held a snow-white lamb in one arm and gestured toward the beholder with his other arm. The committee members stood around the oak table at the center of the room and asked Manny about their new pastor.

"She got a family then?"

"I don't know."

"How old is she?"

"I don't know."

"She know her Bible?"

"I don't know, I suppose."

The outside door opened and the committee fell silent, listening to a man's voice echo in the hallway and a woman's high heels clip-clop against the linoleum. Stiffler, a tall, thin man with pale, sunken cheeks entered the Adult Room, alone. Like John the Baptist, he was preparing the way. He greeted the group, shook each person's hand, then gestured toward the empty doorway and said, "Your new pastor, Reverend Washington." A black woman appeared: tall, fortyish, salt-and-pepper hair. She wore a turquoise business suit, an ivory blouse, and a Navajo necklace of turquoise and silver. John's eyes bulged, his faced flushed. He glanced at Manny.

Stiffler said, "Please – everyone have a seat. This is your time to get to know one another." The Calvary people sat, silent as the Calvary cornerstone laid in 1909. Reverend Washington waited. Finally, Manny spoke: "Ah, Reverend Washington is it?"

"Yes. Edith Washington," she said in a low, rich voice.

"You got a favorite Bible verse?" At least we got the Good Book in common, he thought.

"I guess I do. My daddy, who was a preacher too, made me learn it by heart when I was just a girl. It's from Hebrews: 'The Word of God is living and active, sharper than any two-edged sword, piercing to the division of soul and spirit, of joints and marrow, and discerning the thoughts and intentions of the heart. And before God no creature is hidden, but all are open and laid bare to the eyes of Him with whom we have to do.'" The words of that passage floated around the room like stiff air-freshener. She continued, "Reverend Stiffler tells me you asked for a pastor who can bring in the neighborhood folk. I can bring them in ..." she paused, "... if you really want them. Most of them look a lot more like me than you."

No one spoke, until John elbowed Manny. In a voice which blended perfect defeat with matter-of-factness, Manny said, "We'll be closing the doors soon if they don't come."

Reverend Washington looked at Manny and asked, "You want them enough to make some changes so that black folk will feel welcome here?"

Manny folded his hands on the table in front of him and looked at his black-and-blue thumbnail, a reminder that his aim with a hammer – or a letter to his bishop – was not always good. "Changes? Like what kinds of changes?" he asked, not looking up.

"Like being proud of a black woman preacher. Other changes will come in time."

John spoke up: "Where's your husband?"

Reverend Washington turned to him and considered her answer. "I'm still looking for one."

Mrs. Kolander, a seventy-year-old widow, sighed, let down her shoulders, and said happily, "You and my daughter both!"

Reverend Stiffler did most of the talking for the rest of the meeting. He told about Reverend Washington's experience with bringing blacks into a white church and about Calvary's experience with keeping blacks out of a white church. He concluded by saying, "It's a match made in heaven and confirmed by the Bishop."

Manny opened the front door to his home and shouted, "Where's my Bible?"

Gladys turned away from the ten o'clock news and looked at her husband. She pointed to a stack of magazines and books and said, "In there somewhere. That new preacher put some religion in you, did she?"

Without answering, Manny pulled out a red, leather-bound Bible, put on his reading glasses, licked the tip of his forefinger, and flipped through the gold-edged pages of the Old Testament, looking for Hebrews. "It ain't in here," he said.

"What's that?"

"The Book of Hebrews."

"That's in the New Testament."

"It is?" Manny flipped through the gospels and finally got to Hebrews. Sitting on the couch next to Gladys, he began to read, moving his lips but not voicing any words.

Gladys turned back to the television. The weatherman stood in front of a national map and pointed to a low-pressure area circling a high-pressure area over the Great Plains. "Lots of storms in this mix," he said, "and coming our way."

Manny said, "Thank God it's not in red ink."

Gladys looked at her husband and asked, "What on earth are you talking about?"

"I'm not talking about anything on earth, Gladys. Listen to this." He read the passage out loud with great care, making sure that he correctly pronounced each word. Manny looked at her over his reading glasses and asked, "Have you ever heard that before?"

Gladys shook her head. "Mercy, no. It gives me the willies."

"Our new preacher is a colored woman who can't find a husband and that's her favorite passage." Gladys' eyes opened wide, but she said nothing. Manny held the open Bible in both hands and looked at it as if it were an old friend who had betrayed him, thinking, I wonder what else is in here I never heard of?

On Saturday morning, the phone rang. Gladys answered it, cupped her hand over the receiver and said, "It's her."

Manny raised his eyebrows, took the phone, and said politely, "Yes, hello there, Reverend."

"Brother Schaefer. I would like you to read the scriptures tomorrow." This request put Manny in a tight spot. He regarded a pastor's first request in the same league with a dying man's last request, but he was not a man who liked to be in front of people, preferring to be behind them, which is why he was Head Usher. He knew every member of Calvary by the back of his or her head.

"I got ushering to do, Reverend," he said.

"Ask someone to cover for you this week. The people need you up front tomorrow. And so do I."

On Sunday morning, Reverend Washington and Manny walked to the blond oak altar at the front of the sanctuary and dropped to their knees. When they arose, Manny struck a match and lit the pair of tall, white altar candles. Reverend Washington walked to a carved oak chair near the pulpit, a chair meant to inspire fierceness, with lion-paw arms and legs, a lion-head back, and a purple, velvet cushion. Manny walked to an oak chair near the lectern, a chair meant to inspire modesty, without cushion or carving. He sat and looked at the people in the pews, unaccustomed to seeing their faces rather than the backs of their heads.

The morning sun poured through the stained glass windows, splattering the pews and people with red, blue, green, and yellow light. Gladys sat next to Mildred Hoppel's daughter, Sara. A black man and woman, finely dressed, sat in the pew where John and Ethel had sat each Sunday for the last forty-two years. Manny heard a child sneeze and noticed a young black couple, with four children. He thought, children! in our church! I hope we got enough free bibles for all these visitors!

The organist, Mildred Hoppel's son, Frank, switched on the electronic vibrato and played a warbly verse of "Amazing Grace." Manny looked across the chancel at his new pastor, who wore a black scholar's robe and black pumps. She closed her eyes and swayed back and forth, her body part of the music. Manny closed his eyes too, hoping that when he opened them he would be looking at a real minister – a man, white, like Jesus.

The organ prelude ended. Reverend Washington stood up, lifted her robe like a prom dress and climbed the three steps into the pulpit. She let go of her robe and raised her arms toward the congregation as if gathering them to her. "Good morning, people of Calvary!" she shouted. Unaccustomed to being shouted at from the pulpit, Manny's people pressed against the backs of their pews and looked at one another, confused. A draft flickered the altar candle flames. The only person to say anything out loud was the black man who sat in John's pew, and he said only one word, "Well?" This silence threw Reverend Washington, and she turned her outstretched arms away from the people and toward Manny. "Brother Schaefer, would you lead us in a prayer for our first worship service together?" She spun around, lifted her robe and returned to her lion chair.

No pastor had ever asked Manny to pray out loud for a worship service. What can I pray? he asked himself, panicked. He couldn't use his bedtime prayer, "Now I lay me down to sleep ..." or his favorite mealtime prayer, "Come Lord Jesus be our guest...." What came to mind for him was that passage from Hebrews, which he had read so often that week that he knew it by heart. He stood, walked to the microphone, cleared his throat, and said, "Let us pray.... The Word of God is living and active, sharper than any two-edged sword, piercing to the division of soul and spirit and thoughts and feelings. And before God no creature is hid, but all are open and laid bare to Him with whom we have to do." Gladys stared at her husband, astonished that those words had become his words.

Reverend Washington took strength from his prayer. She regained the pulpit, held her head high and introduced herself. "I'm your new pastor, Reverend Edith Washington. I'm beautiful!" In fourteen years of preaching, her predecessor, Reverend Morgan, had never used the word, beautiful. She added: "You're the people of Calvary. You're beautiful!" Manny blinked his eyes. People had called him many things in his sixty-eight years on earth, but no one had ever called him beautiful. The new preacher did two things right in her first sermon: she did not quote any startling bible verses, and she sang a solo, *a capella* verse of "Softly and Tenderly, Jesus is Calling," in memory of Mildred Hoppel.

After worship, the congregation gathered in Blatherwick Hall for coffee and visiting. The black visitors, along with the Calvary greeters – who had never dealt with such visitor volume – circled Reverend Washington next to the silver coffee urn. Six oldtimers approached Manny, led by John's wife, Ethel. She walked up to Manny until the sharp tips of her royal-blue high heels almost touched the rounded toes of his beige Hush Puppies. Manny, like John, feared Ethel.

Ethel snorted like an angry mare and said, "How could the bishop do this to us?"

Manny pointed at the crowd of people around their new pastor. "Didn't we want a pastor who could bring in some new blood?"

"We didn't want a colored woman and you know it! Either she goes or we go." Ethel turned and walked away.

Manny and Gladys made their way down the steep, concrete stairs just outside Calvary's front door. He opened her car door, shut it behind her, and got in on his side.

Gladys said, "I talked to her a little. She seemed real nice."

Manny turned his head toward his wife and asked, "Could you get used to her, a colored woman and all?"

Gladys smiled and said, "I got used to you, didn't I?"

Manny started the car, revved the gas like he used to when he was a young man courting Gladys, and said, "Of course you did. I'm beautiful!"

People phoned Manny that week. Mrs. Peters, the chief

money-counter, said, "We had a hundred dollar bill in the collection plate. That's the first time I seen Mr. Franklin's fine face in a long while." Mr. Schmidt, head of the parsonage committee, called Manny and said, "That new Reverend of yours wants a dishwasher in the parsonage. Who does she think she is? We ain't got enough money to buy her a pair of Playtex gloves!" Manny listened to each caller without saying much. He was sad and quiet, like he had been after Mildred Hoppel's funeral. Ethel called on Friday, and after listening to her for a half an hour, Manny said, "I don't know what to do." This too, was a prayer.

Before going to bed on Saturday night, Manny stood in front of the bedroom mirror. He didn't look beautiful. He looked old and tired, a little under the weather. I'll be the next one in a casket at the front of the church, he thought. And guess who'll be preaching over me? With his fingertips, he explored the lymph nodes under his jaw and stuck out his tongue. He thought it looked white so he cracked the seal on the Pepto Bismol bottle, filled a tablespoon with the thick pink juice, and lifted it to his mouth. About midnight, the storms from the Great Plains moved over Milwaukee. Rain, driven by a stiff west wind, pelted Manny's bedroom window, and thunder rattled the tablespoon which he had left on the bathroom counter.

That next morning, Reverend Washington mounted the pulpit, raised her arms, and shouted, "Good morning, people of Calvary!" Manny nodded his head and lifted his hand off his lap, wanting to acknowledge her. Reverend Washington kept her arms raised, welcoming the silence which followed. Again, she turned to Manny and asked him to pray for the worship service. This time, he was ready. He walked to the lectern and said, "Let us pray." He watched his people close their eyes and bow those heads he knew so well from behind. He knew that John and Ethel were attending Good Shepherd Lutheran Church, on Center Street. Manny closed his eyes and said, "Dear Lord, we are proud of our new pastor, Reverend Washington, and we pray that she speak a good word for Jesus."

FAMILY VALUES

I SAT IN THE BACK SEAT, closed my eyes, folded my hands, and prayed to my Father in Heaven that my father on earth would not turn left, but he did, as he did each Sunday on our way home from church, parking along the curb in front of the side-by-side Milwaukee flat. "I don't feel too good," I said. "Can't we go home?"

Mom turned around in her seat and looked at my face. "He looks a little pale," she said, laying her forty-year-old palm against my nine-year-old forehead, checking for fever.

"We'll only stay a minute," Dad said, getting out of the car.

The three of us walked up to the oak front door, its varnish blistered, its veneer rippled and cracked. Dad opened the door without knocking, turned, and waited for us to enter, as if he were still greeting at the church door. Mom entered first, her feet wobbling in high heels. I put my head down and walked into the overheated living room, which smelled of boiled meat, cigar smoke, and pee. Grandpa sat in his gold easy chair, twin chins against his chest, eyes shut, swollen right leg lying on the hassock like a patient on a stretcher. He wore baggy beige pants and a scoop-necked tee-shirt which stretched over his water belly and only half-covered the weed patch of hair on his chest. Dad stepped in behind me, closed the door, and yelled, "Wake up!"

Grandpa grunted, lifted his head, and said, "Oh! Look who's here!" He pushed himself out of his chair and limped toward us, acting surprised to see us, though he could have set his clock by our Sunday visits.

Grandma appeared at the top of the stairs, checking the shape of her hair with delicate pats from her cupped hand. She wore her Sunday house-dress, a loose, white pullover printed with hundreds of tiny red strawberries, fuzzy red slippers, and seamed nylons which bagged at the ankles. When she grabbed the metal stair-rail and began her descent, we stood and watched her in silence, the same way we had watched Reverend Kruger in his black robe process down the long aisle to the altar. She gritted her teeth as she made her way down the last several steps, wanting us to see that she was old and in pain and going out of her way to visit with us. Red sores and brown scabs dotted her arms, protests against her constant scratching. When she got both feet on the floor, she stood still and caught her breath. Dad asked, "How are ya, Ma?"

"I haven't felt well," she said, listing her complaints with bitter delight. "I'd have gone to church today if I'd have felt better." She walked toward me and said, "I love you." She grabbed my ears and kissed me on the lips. Her dress fell away from her chest and I glimpsed her breasts, white flesh pyramids with purple nipples.

I shut my eyes and said, "I love you too Grandma."

We sat in the same chairs each week. I pulled the folded

church bulletin from my shirt pocket and studied the pencil figures I had sketched during the sermon – a fat Tarzan swinging from a vine about to snap, a skinny Jesus with long hair and robe walking down a road, alone. Dad looked at Grandma and said, "Is that son of yours going to come downstairs?"

"Your brother's taking a bath," she said defensively. We could hear bath water filling the upstairs tub. Uncle Fred had received a degree from a commercial art school but, unable to find work as an artist, he had traded in his paints and brushes for an adding machine and typewriter and had become a warehouse secretary. I didn't know much else about him except that he bought a new hardtop Impala every other year and spent weekends in his upstairs bedroom, a room I had never seen. He came down to visit with us only on Christmas and Easter. Each time I saw him, his black curly hair was shorter, his stomach bigger.

Grandma, patting her hair again, frowned, looked at me, and said, "Would you be a dear and get my hairbrush? It's on the vanity in my bedroom." I glanced at Dad and he nodded, so I climbed the stairs, walked past the closed bathroom door, the closed door to Uncle Fred's room, and into their bedroom, which smelled like talcum and perfume. I touched the soft pile of quilts on the dark wood bed as I walked by it. Grandma's vanity was like a little drug store with rows of bottled skin cream, cosmetics, salves, pills, and perfumes, all doubled in the tall, narrow mirror. I noticed an old black-and-white photo pressed under the vanity glass and first thought that the man in the photo was my dad, tall and slender with straight black hair, decked out in a black tuxedo. With one arm he held a violin, with the other he held a slender, young woman. She wore a long dress which hung below her knees and a hat with a little face-veil which covered her forehead and eyes, making her large, dark lips really stand out. I studied their faces and it hit me: It's them! Long, long ago!

Hairbrush in hand, I stopped alongside the bathroom door and listened to my uncle splashing in the tub, then turned and opened the door to his bedroom. The room was tidy and bright, with blue curtains, matching bedspread, and a Zenith color television. I wanted to see his view of the neighborhood so I moved to the window. A robin flushed from a window-sill nest of mud and grass, leaving exposed her four blue eggs. The perfect family, I thought. Eager to see what Uncle Fred kept under his bed, I turned, dropped to my belly, lifted the bedspread, and pulled a black cardboard box from under the bed. What's this? I wondered. I opened it and looked at the row of labeled, metal tubs lined up like soldiers – oil paints! Unscrewing the black cap from one tube, I touched my tongue to the bitter red paint on the inside of the cap. Uncle Fred sloshed in the tub, making me think he might be getting out, so I recapped the tube and slid the box under the bed.

Back in the living room, I handed the brush to Grandma just as Dad said to her, "Every time we visit, that son of yours is taking a bath!" He got up from the couch, walked to the bottom of the stairs and cupped his hands around his mouth to make a bullhorn. "Hey!" he yelled, "You going to visit with your nephew for once in your life?" No reply. "Women take baths. Men take showers!" No reply.

"Leave him alone," Grandma ordered. Dad loosened his tie, walked back to his chair and sat down. Grandma said,

"He's going to take us for a drive in the country this afternoon in his new car."

Dad got angry again. "Ma, you were too sick to go to church. You should be too sick to go on a drive!" Dad gestured toward us, "Even your grandson can see through your excuses." His mother hadn't gone to church in twenty years. She gritted her teeth, unable to reply. No one spoke.

Grandma set down her hairbrush, turned to the end table, and picked up a large white box. She removed the cover and asked, "How about a chocolate-covered cherry?" She stood up, slowly, and offered the cherries to my mom as faithfully and gravely as the church ushers had offered us the brass collection-plate earlier that morning. I half expected to hear organ music. She started to walk toward me but stopped and looked at Grandpa. "You fat old pig," she said. "I pass these out every week while you just sit there. You pass them out today!" Every Sunday, she found a way to call him a fat old pig in front of God and family, and he did not object. For this, I hated them both.

Grandpa got out of his chair and took the box from her. He waited for her to sit down and lowered the white box in front of her. Struck with abundance, she proudly looked up and down each row of cherries and finally took one from a corner. "Thank you," she said, politely. A drop of sweat broke my hairline and dribbled down my forehead. The little red arrow on the wall thermostat pointed at eighty. Grandpa offered the box to Dad and lastly to me. I didn't take one right away because I was afraid that Grandpa would see my hands shaking. "Go on, Sonny," he said. I took one dark-chocolate cherry from its ruffled paper nest and held it between my fingers. My stomach churned. Grandpa put the cover on the box and sat.

I stood and said, "Grandma!"

She turned her head toward me and said, "Yes, dear?" The chocolate cherry smashed against her forehead like a bug against a windshield and she fell against the back of the couch, eyes rolling wildly, silent. The bright red cherry slid to a stop against her glasses, its red juice running down the side of her nose. Melted chocolate stuck to my fingers. Mom ignored me and rushed to Grandma. Dad ignored Grandma and came for me, but I beat him out the front door. I ran down the sidewalk, past clipped, green lawns, past evergreens trimmed into perfect globes and pyramids, past brick houses as square and solid as Reverend Kruger. What goes on in those houses? I wondered. I saw patches of yellow, the tiny faces of daffodils. They're looking at me! I thought. They must know how rotten I am!

A shout behind me: "Sonny!" I looked over my shoulder and saw Grandpa chasing me, his belly and breasts bouncing. I yelled, "Catch me if you can, Hippo!" When Dad chased me, I ran for my life, but I did not fear Grandpa.

For three blocks, he chased me. I stayed a few steps ahead of him and listened to his heaving breaths, his slippers scraping the sidewalk. His arms and hands slapped the sidewalk when he fell. I stopped and turned. Frightened, I ran to him and knelt by his blubber body. He lay on his back, his mouth a bucket, sucking air. I buried my face against his stomach and sobbed, sure that he was dying, sure that his death would be my fault.

His mouth closed. His breathing eased. He turned his

head, looked at me, and smiled.

"I didn't know you could run, Grandpa," I said.

"I can't."

Do you still have your violin?" I asked.

Surprised, he looked at me. "Who told you about my violin?"

"I saw you holding it in a picture."

He rose to his elbows, rested, sat, rested, got to his knees, rested, stood.

We walked back, his arm around my shoulder, past the deep-green lawns, daffodils, trimmed evergreens, quiet houses, past Dad, who stood on the front porch and said to me, "You're going to get it," past Grandma, who sat on the couch, fanning her face with a magazine, still attended by Mom.

Grandpa opened his bedroom closet door, bent inside, and threw boxes and shoes into the room like a badger throwing out den dirt. He turned to me with a black leather case and said, "Open it." I set the case on the bed, unlatched the clasps, and opened the top. The violin reminded me of a tiny, finely shaped woman, wearing grain swirls, black inlay, and heavy strings.

He found the bow in the closet and said, "It's strung with horsetail. When I used to play, I'd picture a horse running free, kicking high."

He pressed the violin into the folds of his rooster neck, pulled the bow across a tightly wrapped string, and created a dry, warbly sound, like a woman singing a single note with shallow, unsteady breath. He lifted the bow from the string and blinked his eyes. I heard a cough behind me and turned.

Uncle Fred stood in the doorway, in his blue bathrobe. Grandpa squeezed his eyes shut and ran his bow across each string, tuning them. When he found the right tone, his eyes opened, his face relaxed. Soon, Mom, Dad, and Grandma came up the stairs and pressed into the narrow hallway behind Uncle Fred. To himself, Grandpa said, "Let's see if this fat old pig can still make a little music."

DOWN TO EARTH

M**r. S**teinhafel, a fat, short, city man with a hook nose and bulging eyes, pulled a folded, white handkerchief from his shirt pocket, dabbed the beads of sweat from his fleshy forehead, and looked Steve up and down. He liked what he saw – a man's body, a boy's face, bluewater eyes, a pack of Luckys wedged between white tee-shirt sleeve and strong arm, baggy jeans cinched at the waist with barn twine, work boots covered with dust, heels dug in, braced for a reply. Steinhafel said, "Lots of farm boys want to work for my circus. "Why should I hire you?"

"I can work. I know animals."

"How old are you?"

"Eighteen."

"Sing the 'Star-Spangled Banner' for me."

This threw Steve. "I didn't say I could sing. I said I could work."

"Go back to your farm, kid," the circus owner said, turning to walk away. Steve wet his lips with a curl of his tongue, took a breath and started the anthem, "Oh, say...." Steinhafel stopped. Steve started again, a few notes higher. "Oh, say can you see, by the dawn's early light. What so proudly we hailed at the twilight's last gleaming...."

"Four hundred a month. We go south in October, town to town, just like up here. No drinking before or during work. Do what I say. Got it?"

Steve nodded. "What will I be doing?"

"Helping Johnny with the animals, but I got you in mind for a promotion if I like your work. When can you start?"

"Today."

"Tell your mama and papa goodbye. Be back by six."

Steve sat at the kitchen table, across from his parents, each of them holding a clear glass of cold milk, his ten-year-old sister, Jen, peeling potatoes over the sink. "I got hired by the circus," Steve said. "I need to pack and get on my way."

His parents glanced at one another, bewildered. His sister set down her knife. His dad asked, "I thought you was joining the Army?"

"This is better. I'll see new places and can quit anytime." Jen's eyes swelled with tears. She put her hands over her mouth and ran out the screen door, which banged shut behind her.

"You broke her little red heart. She'll miss you awful," his mom said. Resigned to losing her son, she asked, "What will you be doing?"

"Taking care of the animals."

"What kind of animals?"

He shrugged. "Whatever they got."

His dad gulped the last of his milk, set the white-coated glass on the table, and asked, "Your mind is made up then?" Steve nodded. His dad got up from the table and went outside. Steve watched him walk to the barn.

His bulging suitcase in hand, Steve returned to the kitchen and looked at his mother. She walked up to him, raised her heels off the floor, and kissed his cheek. "You write. And call – collect – if you need anything."

Steve set down his suitcase inside the open tractor door and looked into the dark barn. He could not see his dad, but he could hear him throwing hay bales in the loft. He shouted, "Dad?" No answer. "I got to go!" Steve turned away from the barn, thinking, he's ashamed I want circus work more than farm work.

Steve cut across the alfalfa field, climbed the fence, and walked into town on the hot asphalt road. Crossing the Sheboygan River bridge, he set down his suitcase, smoked a Lucky, flicked the glowing butt into the river, and watched the current slowly carry it out of sight, wondering when this restlessness in him would quit and he could return to Kiel and the farm life he knew so well.

Mr. Steinhafel took Steve to a long trailer wrapped in sheets of riveted, gleaming aluminum with a row of tiny round windows. Steve thought, looks like a ship on wheels. Steinhafel knocked on the door, and when no one answered, he opened it for Steve and said, "Home sweet home. Take the bed above the cab."

The two left the trailer and walked between the tent and four big rigs lined up alongside one another, the panels of each truck painted with red, white, and blue circus scenes. Near the main entrance to the tent, another truck was parked, its side panel lowered to become the floor of a iron-barred cage. In the cage: a rhinoceros, on its side in the hot sun, worn horn shoved against the bars, legs like stumps. Steinhafel walked up to the cage and said to Steve, "Bought her from a zoo in Alabama. Costs me plenty to lug her ass around but she draws a crowd." He dabbed his brow again. "Johnny don't care much for her so she's yours to keep. I want her and her truck kept spotless. Hose her down before each show. Feed her a bale of hay and a bushel of whatever old vegetables you can find each morning. You can get in there with her but don't turn your back on her."

Steve was bothered by her small cage and defeated body. "She ever get out of there?"

"Ain't been out of that truck since I got her."

"She got a name?"

He shook his head. "Tonight, you just sit in the bleachers and watch the show, watch how it all happens." Steinhafel shouted at two men and joined them, pointing at the tent, giving orders.

Steve studied his new keep. The folds of heavy, rough hide rose and fell with her breath. Her black eyes blinked. Her donkey ears twitched. Her cage stunk. He found a snow shovel, unlatched a side door to the truck and climbed into the hot trailer-truck and into her cage. "Sweetheart. You sure can drop a pile of shit," he said, sliding the shovel underneath the pile.

Steve found a seat on the aluminum bleachers, away from anyone he knew in the crowd – mostly young parents with squirming children who kept their eyes on two fat, caged tigers on the other side of the empty ring. The circus had rented land from a farmer Steve knew – Arnold Bucholz – and had set up in his sheep pasture. Steve noticed the dried, squashed sheep-shit underfoot and the trapeze ropes and cables and swings above the ring. An old man with a big voice and gray mustache walked back and forth in front of the bleachers, shouting, "Get your hotdogs and popcorn before the show starts! Fresh and hot!"

At 7:30, Steinhafel – dressed in a black tuxedo – threw open a tent door, ran to ring-center, raised his arms, and half-shouted, half-sang, "Ladies and Gentlemen!" The crowd quieted, and a gust of wind rolled the tent top like a wave. "You are about to witness Steinhafel's Circus – the finest Small Circus On The Planet Earth! Death-Defying Stunts! Ferocious, Wild Animals! Clumsy's Clowns!" He paused and turned toward a tall opening in the tent wall. "And now, from the faraway land of India – Vishnu and Krishna, along with Johnny Cool, the world's finest wild animal trainer!" Two elephants plowed through a canvas curtain and plodded into the tent, followed by a bare-chested man dressed in tight white pants, black knee-boots, and a wide black belt. In one hand, he held a long metal hook. The elephants lumbered into the ring, and at the man's sharp commands, they rolled over, spun in circles, and sat on stools, showing their great, grey bellies to the crowd. When Johnny raised his arms above his head, Vishnu and Krishna raised their trunks and trumpeted, a shrill noise which made the children in the bleachers squeal and clap but made Steve flinch. The high-pitched noise sounded desperate to him.

Johnny Cool chased the elephants out of the tent while Steinhafel led the crowd in applause and four men set up a ring cage with sections of tall, aluminum bars. Cool strapped on his black holstered handgun, picked up a black whip, and ran to the tigers' cages. He cracked his whip over the pacing animals and they crouched, flattening their ears. The crowd quieted while Cool swung open the doors to both cages, and the tigers bolted to ring center and jumped onto their stools, their striped tails raking across the grass like scythes. The animal trainer joined Steinhafel in front of the cage and turned his bare back to the crowd. Steinhafel pointed at Cool's back and asked the crowd: "You see these scars?" Steve leaned forward in his seat along with everyone else and studied the long, pale welts. "A tiger once attacked Mr. Cool and clawed his back to shreds! Took five hundred stitches to close him up!"

The show lasted forty minutes and Steinhafel introduced each act at just the right moment with just the right words. He used the tone and pace of his words first to rouse, then quiet the crowd. Steve thought, this guy knows how to work a crowd.

Steve slept little that night. Sometime after midnight, three men, drunk and loud, came into the trailer and played poker on the fold-up table before getting into their beds. Johnny Cool came in late, quiet as his big cats.

Early the next morning, the men of the circus took down the tent and bleachers. The crew knew the routine so well that no one spoke, except for Cool, who shouted one-word commands at the elephants as they lowered the fifty-foot center pole. Steve helped load the circus animals into the trucks, but he didn't have to load the rhino – he just prodded her into her truck trailer, collapsed the iron bars, and winched the cage floor back into position as a truck side-panel, which was decorated with a red, oversized painting of the rhino.

Just before noon, the big rigs and trailers pulled onto the highway and drove to Wausau, Wisconsin, for six shows, two a day. He sat in the cab of the rhino's truck without speaking, watching Johnny work through the gears.

"You got a girl back there?" asked Johnny.

Steve lit one of his Luckys and looked into the rear-view mirror at his town. Sadness swelled his throat. "No. But I got my whole life back there."

"Life ain't nowhere except where you're at." Johnny glanced at Steve. "You get lonely – you pay Sylvia a visit."

"Sure ain't no farm wife, is she?" Steve said, remembering how Sylvia had entered the tent on the backs of two white stallions named Ice and Snow, a bare foot braced against each of their backs, her legs, her breasts bouncing under the glittering, sequined vest, arms and smile reaching for the tent top.

"Johnny, why ain't the rhino in the show?"

"Ain't trainable."

"She ever get mean with you?"

"Not yet."

Each time the circus moved to a new town, Steve walked up and down the main drag, comparing it to Kiel's Main Street. Often, he ate lunch at a town cafe, sitting at a counter stool or in a booth, listening to the farmers talk crops and livestock, wondering why he couldn't be like them and stay on the farm. Once, he invited Johnny with him, but Johnny said, "Thanks. I seen enough towns."

In Columbus, Wisconsin, Steve found a library and looked in the card catalog under "Rhinoceros." In the stacks, he found a hardcover book entitled *Africa's Big Five*, a book with stories and black-and-white photographs of elephants, lions, cape buffalo, leopards, and rhino. He found a double-page photo of a black rhino with three white birds on its back, alert, unafraid, standing in knee-high savannah grass. How strong and fine she looks, Steve thought. She's at home and knows it.

Six towns and thirty shows later, Steve knocked on the screen door to Steinhafel's Winnebago and entered. The circus owner sat at a tiny desk cluttered with letters, bills, and a large gray adding machine with green and white keys.

"Johnny said you wanted to see me."

"You like my circus?"

"I like my work," he said, which was true, but he disliked the men he lived with – except for Johnny – and the way the circus animals were treated.

"Johnny says you got that rhino following you around her truck like a farm hog." He pointed to two black tuxedos which hung near the door. "You want to wear one?" Steve wrinkled his brow, confused by the question, and Steinhafel laughed. "Kid, I'm offering you a promotion – I'll work you into my role as Master of the Circus." He frowned and pointed at his throat. "Doctor said I got growths on my vocal chords and should rest my voice or I might lose it. You got to be my voice for a while."

This flattered Steve, but he had misgivings. "I'm no showman. I ain't been up front of a crowd much."

"I can teach you what you need to know. I'll even teach you a southern accent to use down south. Another fifty a month." Steve lifted his eyebrows. "Is that a yes?"

"Can I still work the animals?"

"Done. Take that tux to Sylvia. She'll tailor it to fit."

Carrying the tux across his arm, Steve took a deep breath and knocked on Sylvia's trailer door. Sylvia's dark beauty and reputation unnerved him. He had spoken to her only twice – about her stallions, which he fed, watered, brushed, and exercised each day. She appeared behind the screen door in a white terrycloth robe, brushing her long black hair. "Miss Sylvia," he said. "Mr. Steinhafel said you'd tailor this for me."

Sylvia nodded and held the door open for him. She sat on the rumpled white sheet on her bed and looked at him. "Well?"

"Well what?" he asked.

"Put it on. I won't look." She turned away from him and began brushing her hair again. "The old man's got big plans for you." Steve unlaced his work boots, took off his jeans, and put on the black pants and jacket.

"Okay," he said, holding the baggy pants up with one hand and half wishing she would have turned around earlier, seen the bulge in his white jockeys and pulled him on top of her.

Sylvia took a yellow-and-black tape measure off her table and knelt in front of him to measure his trouser inseam. Steve watched her robe part across her bare thighs. She looked up at him and he jerked his eyes away, which made her laugh.

The next day, Ice came up behind Steve and bit him in the shoulder, hard. Steve yelled, spun around, made a fist, and punched the stallion in his soft, pink nose – a warning. He knew how to be firm with animals without being cruel. Steve spoke to the startled horse, "You're lucky you didn't try that with Johnny. He'd have whipped you bloody."

Two days later, Steve was washing down the rhino's cage when he noticed that his keep had turned to face him and began swinging her head back and forth. Steve set down the hose and took a step back. She charged and backed him into a corner, stopping three feet from him. His heart pounding, Steve knelt slowly, shrinking in size. He picked up a soft carrot from the truck floor, and put it to her mouth, saying, "Easy, girl. Easy." She put out her hook lip, grabbed the carrot, turned, lifted her tail, shit, and moved to her outdoor cage. "I owe you one," he said. From that day forward, Steve called her Louise, after a cranky, unpredictable aunt. He told Johnny, "She had me. She could have put her horn right through me ... but she spared me."

Johnny laughed and said, "Too bad. Steinhafel could have showed you off as the man with a rhino-hole through his gut." That night – for the first time since he left the farm, Steve phoned his family. He didn't have much to say, but he wanted to hear their voices and he wanted to let them know that he was doing well. After the conversation, he felt so lonely that he went to Sylvia's trailer. She came to the screen door, looked at him, smiled, and said, "Come on in for a beer and we'll see what happens."

Two or three times each week, Steinhafel took Steve into the circus ring and taught him how to use his body and voice to work a crowd, making Steve practice in front of empty bleachers, again and again, saying, "I got to drill ya, kid, until that fear in your eyes is gone." Steve began to refer to the circus owner as "Sergeant Steinhafel."

By October, the circus had made its way – town by town – to Henry County, Kentucky, and Steve had made his way to Master of the Circus. The young, small-town women in the bleachers often applauded the handsome man in the tuxedo and dusty work boots as much as the acts, and black families were now part of each crowd. The circus owner made Steve use a southern drawl for the shows, even though he had told Steinhafel, "Talking that way makes me feel like a fake."

Just before Thanksgiving, the circus reached its winter home, a rented farm pasture outside of Red Clay, Alabama, where the crew set up the tent and created new acts for the next season. This off-season was created by Steinhafel's wisdom that "No one thinks circus from Thanksgiving to New Year's."

On Thanksgiving Day, Sylvia and the other women cooked turkey and ham for twenty-two, and the men set up card tables and chairs in the circus ring. After dinner – and before anyone got drunk – Mr. Steinhafel gave his State of the Circus Speech, which Johnny called "The Where We've Gone Wrong But How We Can Be Better Next Year Speech." After the fifteen-minute speech, Steinhafel gave a red envelope to each of his crew and said, "The more I make, the more you make." Steve pictured the circus owner furiously punching the keys of his adding machine, coming up with the precise bonus of $309.83 for each employee. A handwritten note of thanks was included with a check in each envelope, except for the three clowns, who got notes which read, "Your services are no longer needed. Good luck." Steve thought about Thanksgiving dinner on the farm: Uncle Fritz and Aunt Louise'll be there, Dad'll say grace, Mom'll jump up and set out the food, Jen'll be eyeing the pie and cake. I wish I could bump my shoes together like Dorothy, say there's no place like home, and be home. He looked down at his work boots and retied each boot lace.

After the New Year, the circus got moving again – north – with three new clowns. Each act had been reworked, but no new acts had been added. Johnny Cool had tried to talk Mr. Steinhafel into buying a pair of zebra colts from an exotic game farm in Texas, saying, "Zebras are flashy, small, easy to train. We couldn't lose." Steinhafel had shown some interest until he found out that the pair cost three grand.

By mid-July, the circus was back in Wisconsin, just outside Mukwonago, and the rhino gave up. She lay in her truck day and night, eating little, refusing to rise and walk onto her porch cage where people could see her. Alarmed, Steinhafel pressed Steve: "She's your keep. Find out what's wrong with her."

Steve phoned the exotic animal vet at the Milwaukee County Zoo and talked him into visiting the rhino. Steinhafel said, "Good," wiped the sweat from his brow, then frowned, "How much will it cost me?"

Steve took the vet, a man of fifty carrying a stainless steel suitcase, into the hot trailer. Louise lay facing them, her legs bent under her as if she had collapsed, her two-hundred-pound head resting against the metal truck floor. The vet asked, "What about restraints?"

Steve said, "She won't give you no trouble." The vet set down his case, knelt beside the rhino, and examined her eyes, mouth, pulse, and feet, asking Steve about her diet, care, and age. Steinhafel joined the men, standing a safe distance behind them.

The vet said, "I don't think she's sick."

"Tell us what you do think," Steinhafel said, wanting more for his hundred bucks.

The vet turned around and said to him, "I think she's old. Depressed. Tired of living alone and being hauled all over creation."

Irritated, Steinhafel said, "Hell – so am I, but I don't just give up."

Steve, remembering the photo of the rhino on the savannah, said, "She wants to go home and die."

Steinhafel glared at Steve. "She's your keep. Do something."

After the evening show, Steve tossed meat scraps to the tigers while Johnny padlocked their cages for the night and both men returned to the trailer. Johnny asked, "A burger sound good?" Steve nodded and Johnny took a package of ground meat from the tiny refrigerator, pulled it in half, rolled each half into a ball, and flattened each ball between his hands.

"Johnny – how long you been in the circus?"

"Been with Steinhafel ten years. Before that, I drifted from circus to circus." He put the burger patties into a cast-iron skillet and turned the gas on so high that the circle of blue flame roared.

Steve asked, "You like the circus?"

"It's a life."

"Maybe I ain't cut out for this life."

Johnny looked at his young companion. "You do good circus work, kid. But you still ain't decided if you're one of us." Burger grease sizzled and popped in the skillet.

Two weeks later, the circus returned to Arnold Bucholz's sheep pasture, just outside of Kiel. That evening, Steve walked into town and paused on the bridge. River's low this year, he thought. He heard a laugh under him and leaned over the guard rail. Two boys sat on the big rocks under the bridge and watched their red-and-white bobbers float, tilt, drift. Steve dropped his cigarette butt near their bobbers and the boys looked up. "You the Habbeger boys, ain't ya?" They nodded. "You going to the circus?" They nodded again. "Go to Tommy in the ticket booth and tell him you're a guest of Steve Eberly. You'll get in free."

At the farm, Steve stood at the screen door, looking in. He saw his sister look up from her supper plate and point at him, shouting, "He's here!" Without turning around, Steve's father reached out and slammed his hand down in front of Steve's empty chair, his way of inviting his son to join them. His mother got another dinner plate and setting. Jen began to ask her brother questions she'd been holding in for a long time. "You still got them tigers you told us about?"

"Come to the show tomorrow and see for yourself."

"They killed anybody lately?"

Steve raised his eyebrows and whispered, "One got away last week, ran into town, killed a hundred people before we got her back in her cage." His sister's eyes widened with delight.

His mother said, "So you've learned to lie with a straight face now?"

Steve was nervous about the Saturday shows, knowing that he'd look out at the bleacher crowds and see faces he knew. He knew that many envied his travels and work, but he felt foolish in his tuxedo and felt awkward introducing Sylvia and her Stallions, knowing his mom and sister were in the crowd and that his father was not.

After the show, Steve and Johnny Cool returned to their trailer after chores and played five-card stud until the bottle of Jim Beam between them was empty. "You're damn lucky tonight," Steve said, after losing twelve straight hands and eighteen dollars.

One of the clowns, a small man with dark, greasy hair, came into the trailer. "Deal me in," he said, slapping a money clip of bills on the table.

Steve said, "Forget it."

"I said deal me in!" the man repeated, angry.

Disgusted, Steve said, "Go to bed and sleep it off!" Both stood, ready to fight.

Johnny said, "Knock it off. You're both drunk."

Backing off, Steve said, "I think I'll walk around a little." He edged past his adversary, left the trailer without closing the door, and walked around the tent. The tigers growled like guard dogs. At the rhino's truck, he swung open the big doors and looked into the dark trailer. He could not see Louise, but he could hear her breath rattle through her nostrils and knew by its unevenness that she was awake. He hefted an aluminum ramp to the trailer floor. Louise blew twice – clearing her nostrils as she got her legs under her. "Come on," he said, still unable to see her, "let's take a walk." Steve felt the truck give under her steps and saw her worn horn and head emerge from the truck above him. She swung her head, looking, sniffing, and lumbered down the ramp, grunting with each step.

The rhino moved away from the truck and across the dark, soft pasture. Steve got ahead of her, and she followed him like she had learned to do in her truck, right up to Bucholz's closed pasture-gate. Louise waited like a cow for Steve to open the gate. On the gravel drive, Steve turned to her and said, "Feels good to plant them big ugly feet against mother earth, don't it?" When he walked across the highway, the rhino turned and followed the broken yellow lines as if they had been laid for her.

A pair of distant headlights appeared ahead of them, and Steve got alongside her, put his shoulder against her shoulder and tried to push her off the road. Might as well try to push a tank, he thought, amazed at her weight and balance. He could hear the car and squinted into the brightening headlights. Again, he got in front of her and began waving his arms. The white light nearly blinded him before he saw the headlights dip as the driver hit the brakes, slowed, and stopped in the lane thirty feet from him. Louise stopped ten feet from the idling car and began swinging her head from side to side. Jesus, she's pissed off, he thought, she's going to charge! Steve ran to the driver's side of the car and yelled, "Turn off your lights!" Lights off. Steve could now see the driver, a boy of sixteen, mouth open, with his girl by his hip, his arm out the window, both staring at the beast in front of them. Steve said, "Turn off your engine!" The car became as quiet as the night. Louise broke the stalemate by walking past Steve and alongside the car, and Steve followed, getting in front of her again once the car drove away. The asphalt road still held the heat of noon.

He led the rhino down the empty highway, across the bridge outside of town, down County CC. He saw the dark shapes of trees, silos, and barns he knew, and smelled freshly cut hay and moist, rich soil. Crickets chirped along both sides of the road. I hope to God the farm dogs don't get wind of us, he thought.

Steve saw the dark shape of his house and a light in Jen's bedroom window. He knew that his sister loved to lie in her bed with the window open, listening to the whirl and buzz of night insects against the screen, reading adventure stories late into the night. Louise followed Steve down the long gravel drive, under the old elms and maples, past the raspberry bushes and pumpkin patch.

Near the barn, Steve trotted ahead of the rhino and opened a gate. Louise stopped at the entrance to the barn-yard pen and squealed, half through her nose, half through her mouth, a piercing, strange sound which made Steve flinch. Jen put down her book and went to her bedroom window. "Go on," Steve said to Louise, and Jen recognized her brother's voice.

Steve shut the gate behind the rhino.

"What are you doing?"

He jumped at the sound of his sister's voice behind him. "Jesus, girl, you scared me to death."

His sister looked past him and listened to the animal blowing. "What is that, some kind of horse?"

"Look again." Jen moved to the gate.

"Your rhino?"

"Louise."

Thrilled, she said, "You brought your rhino for a visit?"

"Something like that."

"Dad won't like this visit."

"No."

"Hide him."

"Where?"

"In Fenny's old stall." They got the rhino into one of the stalls which their dad had once built for his team of Morgans, Fenny and Fronny.

Steve walked back to the circus in the dark and knocked on Steinhafel's trailer door just as pink and orange light swelled from the horizon behind the circus tent. When the circus owner opened the door, Steve said, "Mr. Steinhafel, I got to show you something about your rhino."

"You got her on her feet?" he asked. Steve nodded. Steinhafel put on his maroon terrycloth robe, slippers, lit a cigar, and went to the rhino's truck with Steve. Steinhafel stopped when he saw the ramp and empty trailer. He looked at Steve.

"She's gone."

Steinhafel's face and voice flashed anger. "Somebody took her?"

"I did."

"Is this a joke?"

"No."

"Where is she?"

"Where she can die in peace."

"I could have the cops haul you to jail!"

"Not if I buy her from you, fair and square."

Steinhafel, beginning to recover, studied Steve. "Now let me get this straight. You stole my animal and now you want to buy her?"

"How much?" Steve's seriousness made Steinhafel sense that he could turn this unexpected theft into a good deal – get his young Master of the Circus out of a bind, and get a dying rhino off his hands.

"Two grand. That's what I paid for her."

"Eighteen hundred."

Steinhafel drew on his cigar, looked at Steve, blew smoke, and asked, "Where you getting this kind of money?"

"From you. If I finish the season without taking any more pay, you'll have my eighteen hundred."

Steinhafel, thinking zebra colts, said, "Done."

Jen got up with her dad just after first light, said to him, "I'll help with your chores before I do mine," and followed him to the barn.

His face tightened when he saw the rhino's rump lying on the bed of fresh straw in Fenny's stall. Without taking his eyes off the animal, he spoke: "Explain how this animal got in my barn."

"Steve brought it last night." He walked to the side of the stall, leaned his head over the top board, and studied the animal beneath him.

Steve got back to the farm at breakfast, took a deep breath, opened the screen door, and walked into the kitchen. His family waited for him at the kitchen table, in their places, silent, and Steve sat at his place. His father asked calmly, "Why did you bring that animal here?"

"Cause this is a good place to be. She hasn't eaten in two weeks. She won't live long. She's dying."

His father said, "She's dead." Steve raised his eyebrows, thinking, she's home, back on the savannah. She's free. His father surprised him with a quiet, tender invitation. "I got a hole dug. Let's you and me bury her."

Steve tied a heavy rope around the rhino's rear leg while his dad backed the tractor to the double barn-door. A front-end loader caked with dark soil hung over the tractor's front end. Steve yelled, "Okay!" His dad nodded, let out the clutch, and the rope tightened, first pulling the rhino's leg and hip, then sliding her one-ton body across the straw.

Steve and Jen walked behind the skidding body, and Jen yelled over the tractor chug, "We're going to bury her beside Fenny, so she'll have company." This pleased Steve, though he said nothing until Louise lay on her side in the hole and his dad gouged a bucket full of fragrant soil from the pile next to the hole. Steve shouted to his dad, "Let me do the rest."

By mid-November, the circus had returned to Red Clay, Alabama, and Steve gave the black tuxedo back to Steinhafel. "I'm paid up now. I'll be moving on after Thanksgiving."

"I figured as much. Where to?"

"Back home – get my feet back on ground I know."

Johnny took a circus truck to Texas and returned three days later with a pair of zebra colts. He and Steve built a small corral for them inside the tent and each man gathered a colt in his arms and carried them from the truck to the corral. The two men, side by side, leaned against the corral and watched the colts run, kick, collide, and tumble, their little black-and-white striped bodies moving too fast for their brains. Johnny said, "They's all legs, ain't they? They's my pride and joy." He slung his arm across Steve's shoulders and both knew that this was their goodbye.

Sylvia served slices of pumpkin pie which hung over the edges of the pie plates while Steinhafel gave his annual State of the Circus speech. He concluded by saying, "Our best year since 1967! And 1971 can be even better!" He passed out the red envelopes and surprised everyone by adding a heartfelt handshake as part of the bonus. Steve opened the envelope and pulled out the check: five hundred even. He read the handwritten note: "Come see our circus sometime, kid. Free admission for you and yours."

"Don't go," Inge said.

"I have to lift the nets," Gustav said. "They been out three days."

"Wait till your brother can go with you."

"No telling how long he'll be laid up."

Inge gave up. "God hisself can't change your mind once it's made up."

Gustav left Sand Harbor at dawn, alone. Gulls circled his fishing tug, urging him on with their harsh cries. They knew his boat and the reward which awaited them if they followed him to his nets, twenty miles out, a hundred fathoms down, down where the moon-eyes swam, the sardines of the Great Lakes which Gustav and his brother, Penny, netted, salted, iced, and shipped to New York City. Fair weather clouds floated across the red and purple sky and chunks of drift ice bobbed like half-sunk barrels in the dark green water on that morning of February 9, 1939.

Later that morning, Inge walked her two children to Newport School on a gravel road which ran along the Lake Michigan bluff, and she searched the brilliant horizon where water met sky. Inge had spent much of her married life searching that horizon for Gustav's boat, sick with fear, wondering if he would get off the Lake and lie next to her that night or end up like her Uncle Sven, who had been swept from the deck of his fishing tug by a mountain-wave when Inge was a girl. The Lake had never returned his body and she often dreamt of her uncle, sinking in steel-blue water, face up, eyes and mouth open, trying to speak to her as he went down.

Carl, ten, asked her, "Can you see Pa's boat?"

"No. I can't."

Carl added, "I wish I could be with him today."

"That Lake is no place for children," Inge said, sternly. She discouraged his interest in fishing as if it was an insult to her.

Carlene, eight, asked, "He's coming to the spelling bee, isn't he?"

Inge's voice brightened. "Goodness, yes! Your father is so proud of you!"

From his pilot's cabin, Gustav scanned the gentle swells for his first buoy, set at eighteen miles – two hours running time – from Sand Harbor. He saw the east wind before he felt it. Ahead of him, the swells rippled, darkened, and shifted shape. Moments later, the wind-shift hit Gustav's tug, spraying water against the windows and lifting the bow. He thought, I got to hurry now.

Gustav brought his tug alongside the buoy, slowed, and stepped out of his pilot's cabin onto the open stern. Goldamn wind is cold, he thought. He reached over the side and grabbed the red-and-white buoy flag. Hand over hand, he pulled the net onto his tug without even removing his catch, except for two chubs which he twisted free and tossed to the shrieking gulls.

By the time Gustav reached his second line, a mile further out, the wind gusted to twenty knots, the swells reached six feet from trough to crest, and dark clouds roiled and swirled above him like smoke. It was twenty degrees colder than when he had left Sand Harbor. He took his bare hands off the wheel, crossed his arms, and stuck his hands under his armpits. As if of one mind, the gulls circled his boat one last time and left him. He watched them fly toward land and thought, if I head in now maybe I can beat the drift ice.

Inge felt the wind-shift on her face and stopped suddenly, as if someone had shouted at her. She turned toward the Lake, saw the dark, distant clouds piling up over the water, and stomped her foot like an anxious mare in stall. Back in her kitchen, Inge sat at the table with her hands wrapped around a hot mug of coffee. She watched the bare branches of the backyard maple stir in the wind and thought, there ain't no wind worse than an east wind this time of year.

For two hours, Gustav quartered the waves at check-speed, zigzagging toward Sand Harbor, running into cakes of drift ice which bounced away from the hull as if hit by a snow-plow. He got within sight of Sand Harbor at noon and shouted, "Goldamn anyways!" The harbor was blocked by drift ice, ice chunks packed against one another like huge, jagged bricks, up and down the shore as far as he could see, rising and falling with each swell. Gustav turned north, broadside to the waves. His tug, his thoughts, began to pitch and roll. Gustav's best thought: I bet there's a break in this ice at the mouth of the Mink.

Once, Gustav and Penny had been kept from their harbor

by an ice wall. Unable to get around or through it, the brothers had plowed their tug into the ice blocks as far as they
could, kept the coal stove burning hot, played cards, ate
beans, crackers, and moon-eyes, and waited. Inge had waited
too, uncertain if her husband was alive or dead. A day later,
the wind had shifted and the ice wall had broken apart, free-
ing their tug and opening the harbor. Inge had run down the
Sand Harbor pier and into Gustav's arms, weeping with re-
lief, until suddenly she backed away from him as if from an
enemy, turned her back, and walked off the pier, alone.

Gustav slowed his tug and shook his head. The ice wall,
unbroken, stretched across the mouth of the Mink River like
a breakwater. For a moment, he thought about crossing the
Lake to the Michigan shore or going all the way around the
Door County peninsula into Green Bay where he could find
open harbors, but he shook his head and thought, I ain't got
enough diesel for either – I'll have to sit it out in the ice. He
ran his boat into the ice wall, parting the ice blocks until he
could not go forward or backward, his temporary harbor, a
hundred yards from the desolate pine-and-cedar shore, one
mile from Inge's kitchen.

Inge filled her blue mixing bowl with flour, salt, water, and
yeast, and began to knead, using the weight of her whole
body to press and shape the ingredients into dough. She set
the bowl on top of the oven and covered it with a dish towel.
Inge had fought him about buying the boat, knowing that her
defeat was just a matter of time. "Stick to farming!" she had
told him. "Stay on dry land, where God meant us to be!" In
order to quiet her down, he had said, "I'm not buying it this
year anyway," but the day had finally come when he had

driven her, pregnant with Carl, to Sand Harbor, pointed to a beat-up fishing tug with black hull and white cabin, and said, "She's got two-inch planking and three-inch ribs and can handle just about anything that Lake can dish out." Inge had put her hand on the rise of her belly and wept. Gustav had shrugged his shoulders and said quietly, "I was born with sea legs, Inge. It's in my blood." His father had fished the Baltic coast off Sweden before coming to Wisconsin. A week later, Gustav had taken Inge onto Lake Michigan, her first time on big water, and she got sick the moment they hit the swells. Less than a quarter mile out of Sand Harbor, Inge had pointed toward shore and said, between heaves, "Take me back."

Gustav's tug rose and fell with the swells and the ice blocks ground against the oak hull. In his tug's dark cabin, Gustav crumpled sheets of newspaper and packed them into the little iron stove. He kept the diesel idling. His hands, stiff with cold, awkwardly struck a match against the side of the stove – once, twice, until the match flamed. After lighting the paper and kindling, he turned and lifted the coal-bin cover. One piece of coal the size of his fist lay at the bottom of the bin. He blinked, stunned. He had never thought to fill the coal bin that morning because his brother always took charge of the coal and food. He opened the cupboard above the fish cleaning table: two empty shelves. He struck his forehead with the butt of his palm and said, "I ought to have my head examined. This Lake don't forget mistakes." Gustav tossed the piece of coal into the stove and kicked apart the coal-bin cover. The dark clouds passed, the wind eased, the temperature fell to zero, five below, ten below.

On her cutting board, Inge pulled apart the raised dough into four pieces, rolled each into a loaf, and put each loaf into a greased tin, covering them all with a dish towel. Tossing her apron across a kitchen chair, she walked into the back hall, put on her brown wool coat, and opened the back door. A minute later she was walking through the orchard, between the rows of cherry trees which rose and fell with the slope of the land. To keep her face out of the wind, Inge looked at the ground. The naked branches of the trees clacked against one another, sharply. In her mind, she pictured the orchard in full bloom, still, bees buzzing from blossom to blossom, Gustav and her walking through the orchard at dusk without talking. She lifted her head when she got to the top of the highest hill on their farm and saw the waves break near shore, and beyond, in deeper water, she saw the ice wall. I should have married a farmer, not a fisherman! she thought as she turned her back on the Lake. Had she looked to the south, she could have seen the skinny plume of smoke rising from Gustav's stove.

Back in her kitchen, Inge lifted the dish towel and checked her dough. Three loaves had risen nicely; one not at all. She placed the raised loaves into the oven and sat at the kitchen table, the tin with the flat loaf between her hands, as if the warmth of her hands might encourage the dough to rise. The kitchen windows had steamed and frosted and she could not see outside, so she rubbed an open palm against the window until the ice melted and she could see the driveway through a circle of clear glass. She thought, oh, to see his truck pull into the driveway!

His pickup did not appear but Carl and Carlene ran up the

driveway, their breath steaming from open mouths. They had run all the way from school to keep warm. While they stomped the snow off their shoes in the back hall, Inge looked at them and said, "Look at your cheeks, red as summer cherries!"

Carl saw that the look on his mother's face did not match her bright voice and asked, "Pa's not off the Lake yet, is he?"

"No," she said, looking down, thinking, I guess my face shows everything. Worry lines stretched across her forehead like waves along the beach.

Inge made hot chocolate and sat with the children at the kitchen table. Carl, silent, serious, sat in his father's chair, while Carlene talked about school. "I won our practice bee today," she said. Inge looked through the circle in the frosted window and said nothing.

Carl pushed back his chair, stood, and spoke in a manly voice, "I got chores to do before dark."

"Bundle up then!" Inge warned.

At dusk, the wind quit. The blocks of drift ice froze together as if welded. Gustav sat in the dark cabin with his back against the idling Kahlenberg, a forty-five horse, three-cylinder diesel which put out a little heat and a reassuring chug. At his feet lay the rest of his scavenged stove fuel: shovel handle, four plank shelves, three cupboard doors, fathom string, and two fish boxes which he had kicked apart. He thought, if I can keep that fire going I'll be alright.

Gustav's brother got out of bed for the first time in two days when Inge called. "How's your back?" she asked.

"Not too bad," Penny said.

"Gustav took the boat out by hisself."

"Any other boats go out today?"

"No. I checked. There's an ice wall. He can't get in."

After a long silence, Penny said, "He's got coal and food. If he uses his head, he'll be alright."

That evening, Penny, standing in for Gustav, drove Inge, Carl, and Carlene to Newport School. Two enormous maples, bare as skeletons, arched the entrance to the white frame schoolhouse. Once inside, the children gathered around the big-bellied stove, and the parents and other adults, still in their heavy coats, sat on the children's wooden chairs. Inge and Penny sat next to Hans Olafsen, a bachelor fisherman who ran a boat out of Sand Harbor and who was attending the bee to encourage his niece. Penny explained Gustav's absence to Hans, adding quietly, "I don't like him out there all alone."

Hans nodded and said, "If you want to go out at first light and look for him, phone me. We'll take my boat."

Inge, who usually loved to visit at such gatherings, held to herself and studied the rough-cut ceiling beams, the tall, frosted windows, and the uneven floorboards. Against her will, Inge imagined that she was in the cabin of a ship, the swells tilting and rolling the entire room. She closed her eyes and swayed, sick to her stomach.

Mrs. Nislett, the teacher, arranged the twenty-two children by height in a single row at the front of the room. At eight o'clock, she nodded to Carl and he broke ranks and walked up to the bell rope which dangled from a hole in the ceiling. When Carl jerked the rope, Inge's body tensed. She felt the vibrations of the bell in the floorboards and listened to the peal carry across the frozen land.

From inside his tug's cabin, Gustav heard the school bell. He stood, opened the cabin's door, and walked stiffly onto the open stern. He looked south along the dark shore and toward the school, which he and Inge had attended for eight years. In fifth grade, Inge had sat in front of Gustav and once that year, he had dipped the tip of Inge's long braid into his inkwell and written his name with her wet braid on a piece of paper, later giving it to her. When Inge's girlfriend told her how Gustav had penned the note, she turned around and said to him, "I hate you!"

He imagined his children at the spelling bee and thought, Carlene will be thinking about letters and words. Carl will be thinking about losing to his sister. He tore three frozen chubs from the net and looked up at the sky, bitter black, swept with stars. To the north, green lights, the auroras, fluttered across space like a curtain in front of an open window.

Carl misspelled his first word, foreigner. He frowned, angry with himself, and sat. Carlene correctly spelled her first word and every word she was given until just she and another girl stood at the front of the room, facing the parents and other children. Mrs. Nislett looked at Carlene and said, "Treach-er-ous." The room began to pitch and roll for Inge, her stomach rising to her throat. Just as Carlene began, "T … r …" Inge stood, walked across the uneven wood floor and out the front door. Confused by her mother's exit, Carlene stopped spelling. She heard her mother vomit on the school porch and ran out the front door.

Back in his tug's cabin, Gustav sat on the wood floor with his back against the warm engine. Without warning, the diesel quit and a silence settled around him like a presence, so deep and alive that he became alarmed. He tried to light the warming plugs but he quickly discovered that they were dry: no diesel left, empty. He wanted to shout or swear but he kept silent, knowing that words gave away warmth and energy and he could not afford such a loss. He blew into his hands, stuck a long wood splinter down the gullet of a chub, and roasted it over the little fire in the stove.

Penny helped Inge out of his car and across the dark, frozen yard. Carl pointed to the north and said, "Look!"

"The dancing lights," Penny said.

Carlene asked, "Why do they dance like that?"

Without looking up, Inge said, "To keep warm."

At the kitchen table, Carlene stood next to her mother. Inge, still queasy, forced a smile and asked, "How did you get to be so smart, spelling those big words like that?"

Carlene ignored the question and asked, "Can Carl and I sleep in your bed tonight?"

"I guess so. I'll fix you a hot-water bottle. You go put on the extra quilt." Inge turned to Carl and said, "Stoke the furnace for the night." Thrilled that he had been given one of his father's chores, Carl ran into the basement two steps at a time. He pulled open the furnace door and shoveled four bread-loaf-sized lumps of coal into the furnace. That'll keep us warm all night, he thought as he watched the bed of glowing coals dim, brighten, dim, brighten, pulsing like a human heart.

The children put on their flannel pajamas, threw back the quilts and happily fell onto their parents' bed. They pulled the quilts over their heads, slid their legs down the cold sheet and giggled when their feet met by the hot-water bottle. Carlene dug her longest toenail into the soft bottom of Carl's foot. He shrieked, jerked his foot away and said, "Keep them ugly meathooks to yourself!" They quieted and Carl began to repeat the words to a rhyme which Inge had taught them. Carlene joined him, saying over and over:

Daddy, Daddy, where are you tonight?
The sky is so dark, the Lake is so deep
We miss you when you are far out of sight
Come tuck us in bed and rock us to sleep.

Penny sat at the table in Gustav's chair and studied Inge, who rubbed another circle of frost from the window and looked through it into the dark. He knew then that they would sit there all night, watching the driveway, listening to the rafters crack with cold. After an hour of quiet, Inge said, almost in a whisper, "The Lake is bigger than God. I will ask the Lake for mercy."

Gustav paced back and forth in the dark cabin: the fire, out, his stack of wood, gone. He blew into his hands and pounded his ears but could no longer feel them. Recalling the fluttering curtain of light in the sky, he thought, if I die tonight I'm going through that window to the other side, see what's there.

Back in the kitchen, the percolator gave off happy, gurgling sounds, like an infant in a crib. Penny poured a cup for Inge and himself. She said, "In the dark you look just like him."

Gustav paced back and forth and swung his arms in the tug's cabin. His body seized and clenched from shivers that came from under his heart, his last place of warmth. The thought came slowly, as if the cold had numbed his mind: I'll not last to dawn on this boat. His next thought: I can freeze to death here or I can take a chance – swim, and if I make shore, run like hell!

Knowing that his clothes would slow him down in the water, he began to undress, pushing the suspenders off his shoulders with his wrists. His oilers and trousers crumpled and fell to his knees. Clumsily, he kicked off his boots and pulled off the rest of his clothes. Naked, Gustav stepped out of the cabin, into the night, the silence, and lowered his bare feet over the side of his tug and onto an ice block, still holding onto the tug's side rail. For a moment, the ice held him, but when he let go of the rail, the ice rolled, and he dropped into the water like a weighted fathom line. The frigid water revived him and he swam, eyes open but seeing only black, the ice wall now a ceiling above him.

An hour before dawn, Penny phoned Hans Olafsen and said, "This is Penny. Let's see if we can find him."

"Give me half an hour."

"Pick me up at Gustav's place."

Penny and Inge sat at the table and listened for Han's truck. A bang against the back door startled them. Inge said, "He's here, thank God." Penny turned on the back hall light and opened the door. Gustav's heaving body fell into the back hall across Penny's boots. Without speaking, Penny got his arms under his brother and carried him like a child up the back steps, taking stock of his condition: skin like white wax, as if ready to peel; lips, dark blue, the color of the Lake; feet, torn and bloody from his night run across frozen land. Inge gasped and put her hand over her mouth.

Penny said, "He's half-froze but he ain't dead."

Inge ran upstairs and Penny followed with Gustav. She

opened the door to their bedroom and pulled the quilt off her startled children. Penny lay Gustav on the bed next to Carlene, who, half-awake, looked at her father and burst into tears.

Penny said, "Carl, stoke the fire!" Carl stared at the naked man on the bed until Penny yelled, "Now!" and Carl rolled out of bed and ran downstairs. Without speaking, Penny unbuttoned his wool shirt and dropped his trousers to the floor. Inge unbuttoned her sweater, unclasped her bra, and kicked off her shoes. She lay down alongside her husband, pressing her warm body and legs against his, wondering if his whole body could be brought back to life or whether parts of him – his toes, fingers, ears – might never again be part of him. Penny lay down alongside Gustav's other side and pressed against his brother's body, so frigid that his own body shuddered, wanting to pull back. Carlene, quiet now, stood by the bed in her nightgown, her arms wrapped around herself, shivering, uncertain what to do. Carl tossed lumps of coal into the furnace with his hands until his hands were black and the furnace could hold no more. He ran up the stairs three at a time and got Carlene to lay down on top of her father. He laid alongside his sister, their little chests flattened against Gustav's broad, bare chest. With his toes, Carl grabbed the quilts, pulled them to his hand and covered everyone completely, so that they lay in darkness, their breath rising and falling as if from one set of lungs.

Hans Olafsen walked through the open back door, into the lighted kitchen, and yelled, "Anybody home?"

Doc Tyler, the physician from Sister Bay, arrived at dawn. Inge, in her bathrobe, met him at the back door and escorted him to the bedroom. She nodded toward her bed, where Gustav lay under a stack of quilts, alone, and she said, "We got him quieted down." Feeling like she had done what she could, she added, "I'll be in the kitchen with the men and children if you need me."

The frosted kitchen windows glowed with first light and were so beautiful that no one turned on the overhead light. Inge sliced half a loaf of bread and put the stack of thick slices on the table, along with butter and jam. Penny poured cups of coffee – even for Carl and Carlene – and all five of them sat at the table without looking at one another, without speaking, waiting for the sun to break the horizon, until Penny looked at Hans and said, "I reckon we better bring in Gustav's boat." Hans nodded and both men stood.

Inge said, "You're not going anywhere. Sit down." Her quiet voice carried such restrained violence, and underneath that, sorrow, that the men looked at her, one another, and sat.

Doc Tyler walked into the kitchen and said, "Could be better. Could be worse."

The sun pulled itself out of the Lake and into the sky. The wind shifted to the southwest, and the swells which rolled past the mouth of the Mink River had formed off Chicago, two-hundred fifty miles to the south. Gustav's abandoned fishing tug rose and fell on those swells, carried out into the Lake with the drift ice, toward the other shore.